"Fiction is the truth inside the lie."
– Stephen King

Outside Forces

A Screenplay

By Daniel John Carey

ISBN: 978-1-884702-47-1
First published: 2025

Published by: Oakonic

(

Outside Forces

In 1960, a young woman recently out of prison returns to the mysteriously half-abandoned, remote farming town she grew up in as she's intent on rescuing a family member kept for breeding by a disintegrating fundamentalist cult ruled by a deceptive man and his tyrannical sister entangled in their secrets and suspicions.

"All readers come to fiction as willing accomplices to your lies. Such is the basic goodwill contract made the moment we pick up a work of fiction."
– Steve Almond

The Published Script

This script is not of the standard screenplay format. It has been adjusted for publishing.

Because some people read screenplays as some others read novels – strictly for entertainment – this script is being made available in print.

Screenplays often bump around Hollywood for years, before they are optioned or purchased. Even then they may not be produced – or can take years to go into production.

Sometimes – before filming – screenplays are rewritten to display the talents of the actors hired. What you have in your hands is the version of the script the screenwriter wrote.

Publishing this screenplay allows people interested in entering screenplay contests, and other showcases, a way to read what could be considered a top entry – as this script has been.

Outside Forces was a finalist in The Nicholl Fellowship of the Academy of Motion Pictures Arts and Sciences, a quarterfinalist in the Austin Film Festival Screenplay Competition, a semifinalist in both the Screencraft Fellowship and Cinestory Fellowship, and a finalist in the Ojai Film Festival Screenplay Competition. It was voted by The Grey List to be among the top 40 unproduced screenplays in Hollywood. It has been top 1% on Coverfly, which has listed the script as "Extremely Hot."

The Screencraft fellowship wrote:

"*Outside Forces* is a polished, quiet, deeply moving and personal story. A beautiful and haunting depiction of a secluded community in the process of devouring itself from within. The slow ramping of tension in the environmental storytelling of ongoing decay and rising heat is masterfully done, and serves to connect the audience to the circumstances of the characters. The pacing is consistent and engaging, and does a strong job of employing a slow creep without allowing the plot to drag or circle itself. It demonstrates a strong and intuitive sense for film language and storytelling, and the plot is quite tight in how it is woven together."

Genesis

I began writing what was to be a comically off kilter story about an urban hippie commune set in the 1990s. I centered it around a charismatic weirdo who somehow became the leader of the community.

What my story turned into is vastly different from what I had intended.

Everything about the story changed. Including the location and decade. So did the entire concept. It became far more dramatic and darker. I reset it in 1960 among a disintegrating fundamentalist cult in a remote, half-abandoned, sun baked farming town.

I put the script through the screenwriting workshop I ran for eight years called Screenwriting Tribe.

Because the script received so much attention from a variety of screenplay showcases, people thought it would sell, and be produced. Various people got involved with the script. But, so far, it has not resulted in a film.

As I'm writing this in the summer of 2025, more people are considering it for production.

I am making the script available in print so at least people can enjoy it in this form.

If you have never read a screenplay, know it simply presents what is seen, and what is heard. What the characters think – and otherwise descriptions of their inner voice dealing with how they reason – is left out of a screenplay.

A character's fears, regrets, plans, wants, and memories – and otherwise their thoughts – are the type of writing found in a novel. Screenplays usually avoid wordy, novelesque writing.

I know people who are not in the film industry, but who read screenplays for entertainment the way other people read novels. People I know who are not in the industry kept asking me to read this script. These things are what gave me the idea of making the script available in a printed format.

I hope you enjoy *Outside Forces*.

Daniel John Carey

"The child intuitively comprehends that
although these stories are unreal,
they are not untrue."
– Bruno Bettelheim

Outside Forces

BLACK SCREEN

PRE-LAP: Sounds of random 1960 car and big rig truck traffic rush past on a remote highway.

FADE IN:

EXT. REMOTE HIGHWAY JUNK YARD - CALIFORNIA - DAY

SUPER: "Wicks Corner, California, 1960."

Bashed, twisted, dusty, ruined 1940s-50s cars bake in the scorching, high-desert sun. Among them looms...

a hauntingly mangled, rusted, 1940s church bus, windows gone, roof collapsed. Clearly, people died.

ACROSS THE ROAD

A half-busy truck stop fuel station in front of a diner. A few cars and trucks in its parking lot. A painted sign on the roof: "Food and air conditioning." Beyond it are scrub brush hills, and a distant mountain range.

EXT. TRUCKSTOP/DINER - DAY - CONTINUOUS

A dusty early '50s sedan pulls in, rolls past the trucks. Pulls into a parking spot next to a late 1950s convertible hot rod.

INT./EXT. THE CAR/DINER PARKING LOT - CONT.

Hard determination in her eyes, her shoulder-length hair meets a silk scarf fashionably tied around her neck, AMELIA (mid-20s), in a white blouse. Turns off the engine. Dauntingly stares. Then... A deep breath. Releases it.

1

REARVIEW MIRROR: She checks her lipstick.

Out from the car, Amelia stops before...

her reflection in the window of the hot rod car. She adjusts her blouse tucked into jeans. Checks the silk scarf around her neck.

A trucker fueling up his tank whistles at her.

She ignores him as she heads into the diner.

INT. DINER - DAY - MINUTES LATER

1950s rock-n-roll quietly plays. A couple of road-weary truckers eat at the counter as they side-eye a...

Young hipster couple who feed each other fries.

AT A TABLE: coffee is poured into two cups by worn-out waitress, NANCY (50s), white blouse, skirt, waist apron around her girth. As she sits, she slides one cup to...

Amelia, who adds a sugar cube.

Nancy looks about, as if to check to see who might hear.

> **AMELIA**
> I assure you, I won't bring any problems. I was blamed for things I didn't do. So, I avoid any sort of trouble. I moved out here, for a more... quiet life.

> **NANCY**
> I've hired your kind, before. We don't want any problems here.

> **AMELIA**
> Yes, ma'am.

> **NANCY**
> You can call me Nancy.

That relaxes Amelia a bit.

> **NANCY**
> Some of these truckers can be a little handsy.

> **AMELIA**
> Oh, I know their types.

Assured, Nancy nods.

The young hipster couple passes on their way to exit.

                    NANCY
         Last gal I hired rushed off. Told Bobby -- he's
         the cook back there -- she was heading to
         Hollywood to be an actress.

                    AMELIA
              (cynical giggle)
         Good luck with that.

                    NANCY
         You have a man?

                    AMELIA
         No. And I'm in no hurry for that.

Nancy knowingly nods.

                    NANCY
              (RE: Amelia's neck scarf)
         My niece wears a scarf that way.

                    AMELIA
         Yeah? I kinda like 'em, myself.

Amelia adjusts the scarf.

                    NANCY
         If there's any problem with these men, just
         step away. Bobby and his helper, Lewis, can
         take care of it.

With those points clear, they sip their coffees.

EXT. NEAR REMOTE FARM TOWN - DAY

A coyote scampers across the road.

SUPERIMPOSE: "Haven, California."

In the distance, beneath forested mountains, in a mirage
of shimmering heat is a scattering of small farms.

Among them is barely a town. A white, wooden church
steeple with no sect identity is the tallest structure.

EXT. CHURCH - DAY

Several horses are tied near a water trough in the shade
of an oak tree.

In the dirt lot are dusty 1940s-50s cars, scuffed pickup
trucks, and some rickety horse-drawn carriages.

A raven lands on one of the carriages, and observes.

FRONT OF CHURCH

On the door of the basic whitewashed structure is a...

WOODEN SIGN: "Henceforth, evil, be gone!"

The door opens. Out steps pallid CHARLOTTE KEATON (early 20s), with a day-old, badly bruised eye. Hair in a bun, she's in a drab, ankle-length dress. A baby bump is evident.

She heaves over. Vomits onto the scorched dirt. Dust rises. She wipes slobber onto her sleeve. Seems faint.

THE DOOR: Creaks open. Leaning out is BROTHER ALLEN (late 40s), slight, a sincere but unfortunate face, chopped hair, wrinkly white shirt, dark slacks.

> ALLEN
> Are you okay, Sister Charlotte?

She barely nods "yes" and kindly waves him away.

He doubtfully steps back inside.

Her brow furls as she notices...

BENEATH THE OAK TREE

Saddled horses drink from the trough where, face unseen, a thin, raggedy man, ISAIAH (50s), splashes water over his chopped hair.

Charlotte watches. Some vomit still on her chin. Her gaze turns into a sad stare. A fly lands on her chin. She doesn't seem to notice, or care.

INT. CHURCH - DAY

At the lectern, eyes closed to receive revelation is sneering MINISTER DENNIS KEATON (50), chopped hair, thin, in a sweat-stained white shirt and basic trousers.

> DENNIS
> (eyes open with fury)
> They will have you believe their weak ways of giving in to dark cravings. You must reject the cravings!

He suspiciously eyes the...

congregation. In the front row are several thin, long-haired, bored teenage girls in long, plain, dresses.

> **DENNIS** (O.S.)
> We should not want what we should not have. It
> defiles us, and stains our souls.

In the middle rows among a dozen other men in rumpled
white shirts, and with choppy hair, sits nearly decrepit
GRANDFATHER KEATON (late 70s). Most men are older than 40.
Few young men, and only a couple teenaged boys.

> **DENNIS**
> Reject those of the Outside Forces. They follow
> the wide and wrongful path of sin.

In the back sit several women (teens to mid-20s), in long
dresses. They have young children and some have babies. A
few elderly women. No women in their 30s-50s, except...

Next to antsy, clever-faced RUTH (10), sits stern MILDRED
(50). Hair in a bun. As with all females, in a long-
sleeved dress. Mildred's leery eyes glide to focus on...

weary Charlotte, who sits with kind-faced SAMUEL (7).

> **DENNIS**
> Do not mingle with sinners. They will tarnish
> your mind with evil thoughts.

Behind Charlotte, mousy BETTY (early 20s), sits alone and
stares at the back of the pew in front of her.

Near the podium sits nice-looking BROTHER JEFFREY (40).
With a demeaning smirk, he watches the congregants.

> **JEFFREY**
> (a burst of spirit)
> HENCEFORTH, EVIL! BE GONE!

Sincere-faced Allen and the rest of the men rise.

> **MEN**
> (loudly, in unison)
> HENCEFORTH, EVIL! BE GONE!

Leary-eyed Mildred is pleased by the display.

FOYER - LATER

Congregants reverently file from the chapel passing
Grandfather, Samuel, Charlotte, and Betty, who wait.

Jeffrey and Dennis nod at the married men who pass.

Younger wives and children trail them. Several single men
pass. Followed by the seven, bored teenage girls in their
plain, long dresses.

Women and girls open black umbrellas as they exit. Among them is Mildred, and Ruth, who open their umbrellas as they exit.

Dennis exits as Charlotte, Samuel, and Grandfather trail him. Charlotte opens an umbrella as she exits.

Jeffrey follows with Betty behind him, as she, too, opens a black umbrella.

EXT. HAVEN ROAD/ABANDONED HOUSE - DAY

A tree grows through the roof of a half-collapsed house.

Along the road, a horse-drawn covered carriage passes.

EXT. KEATON HOUSE - DAY

Whitewashed, one-story. Wooden chairs on the porch.

The horse-drawn covered carriage stops.

Grandfather steps down with his cane as Dennis exits and ties the horse to a post. They continue to the house.

Sweaty Samuel jumps down, he turns to wait for...

pallid Charlotte who holds her dress to her knees as she steps down. She wipes sweat from her bruised face and continues to the house with Samuel beside her.

INT. BARN - DAY

A cow eats hay as...

It is being milked by Charlotte sitting on a wooden stool. She's in another drab, long dress. Her black eye partially healed.

Finished, she hands the wooden milk bucket to Samuel, who exits.

Charlotte touches the veins of the cow's fore udder. Then looks down at her own chest. Through her dress, she thoughtfully feels her breasts.

EXT. BACK PORCH - DAY

A large wire cage on a wooden table holds several mice, among shreds of cloth and a water bowl.

By its tail, a mouse is carried by Charlotte, who opens the cage top and drops the mouse inside.

Samuel approaches.

                    SAMUEL
          Is there a new one?

She points to a mouse. He watches it, pleased.

INT. KEATON DINING ROOM - NIGHT

Dennis, Grandfather, and Samuel eat dinner in the candle-
lit room of stark, wooden decor.

KITCHEN

A simple sink and cabinets, a wood burning potbellied
stove, and a table with one chair.

A wet cloth on her forehead, weary Charlotte sits in a
chair near the open window. Her hand on her pregnant
belly. The window view overlooks the small orchard, and
the twilight-lit mountains beyond.

EXT. BARN-LIKE FURNITURE CARPENTRY — LOADING DOCK - DAY

Four fit, middle-aged men use clamps to pick up a log from
a stack of them on an old flatbed truck.

INT. CARPENTRY - DAY

Long planks are cut by men using manual equipment. They
hand them to other men who assemble church pews.

His cane in one hand, Grandfather watches from where he
sits on a bench near the windowed office door. It opens.

Poker-faced TIMOTHY KEATON (40), steps out. Strong, lean.
Unlike others, he wears boots, jeans, and a tattered denim
shirt. As he strides through the carpentry...

Grandfather eyes Timothy.

Workers sneak glances at Timothy as he passes. A couple of
them whisper to each other.

Timothy side-eyes them as he passes.

The workers quiet as they continue with their work.

EXT. KEATON FRONT PORCH - DAY

Her feet in the water of a steel wash tub, her drab dress
pulled to her knees, Charlotte sits in a chair. Her baby
bump evident. Her black eye is nearly healed.

YARD

Samuel uses a long stick to hit a stone across the road. Picks up another stone. As faint country music is heard, he turns.

Timothy's truck slow to a stop. The engine cuts and the music halts. He gets out. Removes a ball and kicks it toward...

Samuel, who kicks it back. They go back and forth with it. As Timothy kicks it past...

Samuel, who runs after it.

Timothy looks to...

Charlotte, who thoughtfully puts her hand on her baby bump.

Realization draws Timothy's face. He slightly nods.

The ball rolls back to him. He picks it up.

>   **TIMOTHY**
>   (hands Samuel the ball)
>   You be good for your Mother.

Timothy tousles Samuel's hair.

Charlotte watches as the sound of the truck door closing, the engine starting, and the music turning on.

Timothy's truck drive away.

Charlotte weeps as her gaze lingers.

INT. KEATON KITCHEN - DAY

A knife slices through an orange and nicks Charlotte's finger. She calmly watches blood drip from the cut and onto a stack of sliced oranges.

She dries her finger on her dress, takes a bloodied half of an orange, and juices it in an antiquated crank press.

DINING ROOM

Orange juice is poured into Dennis's glass by Charlotte.

Grandfather moves his glass forward to be filled.

As does Samuel, but his glass is half full.

                    CHARLOTTE
               (mildly, to Samuel)
          Finish what you have.

Samuel retrieves the glass. Charlotte fills Grandfather's
glass with juice.

KITCHEN

Charlotte sadly stares out the window at the mountains.

EXT. SIDE OF HIGHWAY - FARM PRODUCE STAND - DAY

Watermelons are arranged on a table by GABRIEL (60s), his
weathered face shaded by a wide-brimmed straw hat.

A bug splattered truck pulls to the side of the road. The
engine cuts. The TRUCKER (40s), steps out.

He considers the stacked watermelons.

                    TRUCKER
          Watermelon sounds good in this heat.

He chooses a large melon as Gabriel observes.

                    GABRIEL
          Twenty cents for that one.

The Trucker counts coins and hands them to Gabriel.

                    GABRIEL
          Thank you, sir.

                    TRUCKER
               (picks up the melon)
          People 'round these parts don't say much, do
          they?

                    GABRIEL
          Not much.

The Trucker looks over to the view of Haven miles away,
the scant town nearly lost in the shimmer of the heat
mirage.

                    TRUCKER
          This the town that had that accident?

Gabriel studies him, and slightly nods yes. As if a
realization of his rudeness hits, the Trucker nods and
leaves with the melon.

Gabriel stacks melons as the truck engine starts.

EXT. TRUCKSTOP/DINER - DAY

Truckers fuel up their rigs.

A station attendant in a cowboy hat fuels a truck.

The Keaton family sedan creeps into the parking lot.

INT./EXT. THE CAR (MOVING)/TRUCKSTOP DINER - CONT.

Eyes full of wonder, Samuel looks out the open window.

Charlotte at the wheel, she slows to park. Cautiously
looks around.

>   CHARLOTTE
>   You mustn't mention this to Minister Dennis.

They exit the vehicle. She shades herself with an
umbrella.

Samuel steps up to a big truck and looks up in awe.

The truck's driver approaches.

>   CHARLOTTE
>   (takes Samuel's hand)
>   Come.

The trucker curiously watches...

Charlotte and Samuel as they approach the diner. Samuel
looks back to the trucker with disappointment.

INT. DINER - DAY

Steam rises from a plate of food at the cook's window.
1950s rockabilly music is barely heard. The plate of food
is picked up by Nancy.

She places the plate of food on the counter, in front of a
lone trucker. He hungrily digs in.

At a table, a few truckers converse. One watches as...

Charlotte hesitantly enters with Samuel. She draws down
her umbrella. Their faces sweaty. They curiously look
about, as if all is foreign to them.

>   SAMUEL
>   (quietly, eyes widen)
>   Mother, there's music sounds. Like Uncle
>   Timothy's truck.

He gently waves his hands around, as if to feel the air.

                    SAMUEL
          (quietly)
     Mother, it's not hot in here.

                   CHARLOTTE
          (whispers)
     They have a machine that makes cold air.

Nancy hesitantly approaches, as if perplexed by
Charlotte.

                    NANCY
     Please, sit... at any table you'd like.

Charlotte leads Samuel to a window booth as Samuel
observes Nancy.

                    SAMUEL
     Her legs are showing.

                   CHARLOTTE
          (softly)
     Not everyone dresses like us.

CASH REGISTER: Nancy adds up a bill as she unsurely eyes
Charlotte and Samuel.

OTHER SIDE OF DINER

Coffee is poured for a somewhat sleazy TRUCKER (40s), by
Amelia. Another pretty silk scarf tied around her neck.

                    AMELIA
     Grew up near here. Moved back from Los Angeles.
     I got some family things to take care of.

                    TRUCKER
     Family must be expecting to see a wedding ring
     on that finger, by --

                    AMELIA
          (sweetly)
     -- Would you like creamer in your coffee?

He nods. She pours creamer.

                    TRUCKER
          (RE: the scarf)
     How 'bout you let me see that pretty neck.

She winks, and leaves with the coffee decanter.

The put-off Trucker watches her hips sway.

NEAR THE COUNTER

Nancy stops Amelia.

> **NANCY**
> Listen, the woman with the kid isn't gonna
> order anything. She's one of them... local
> religious crazies.

Curious, Amelia looks toward Charlotte's window booth.

> **NANCY**
> They live in an old farm town through the
> mountain pass. It's creepy. Nobody lives out
> that way, but them.

WINDOW BOOTH: Samuel sits alone as he dabs his finger to touch ice cubes in the water glass. Fascinated.

> **NANCY**
> They never come in here. This one's pregnant.
> Wanted to feel the cold air, she said. I gave
> 'em ice water.

Amelia appears more curious.

> **NANCY**
> She's in the ladies room. When she gets back,
> you can check on 'em. See if they want food.
> But, I have to tell ya, them women aren't
> allowed to have money. So...

Nancy shrugs and steps away.

Amelia curiously observes Samuel.

SMALL BATHROOM OF DINER - CONT.

A fly fights to break free from a spider web at the window screen. A spider approaches, then attacks.

Sweat beads form on Charlotte's face as she leans on the wall and wearily stares at a wire hanger on a wall hook.

She takes hold of the hanger.

She lowers the toilet seat. Pulls up her dress to her waist, pulls down her matronly undies, sits.

Her eyes shut and she whispers indecipherably, as if to pray. Her breath deepens, intensely.

Drops the hanger. Rushes to the sink. Vomits.

She cries as she leans against the mirror. Her breath fogs it and her sweat smears it. Her reddened eyes look at their reflection, as if to beg for comfort.

> **CHARLOTTE**
> (breathlessly pleads)
> Mother... Why did you die?... Mother? I feel evil... Help me, Mother. Please.

She cries as her face smears the mirror.

DINER WINDOW TABLE - MINUTES LATER

Samuel sips his ice water and notices...

pallid Charlotte return to sit. Her flushed face is damp.

> **SAMUEL**
> Were you were crying?

> **CHARLOTTE**
> Mother doesn't feel well.

She takes a paper napkin and pats her face.

> **AMELIA**
> (approaches)
> Charlotte?

Charlotte seems jolted by the stranger knowing her name.

> **AMELIA**
> It's Amelia. I cut my hair short. I --

> **CHARLOTTE**
> Amelia? What're you... I wan... I wanted to feel the... cold air. I. It's the first time I've been here.

Charlotte skittishly looks about.

> **AMELIA**
> It's okay. You can rest. It's hot as hell out there.

Charlotte seems unsure as she looks about the diner.

> **AMELIA**
> It's okay Charlotte. I know it must be strange seeing me. Nobody here'll bother you.

Samuel considers Amelia's uniform.

                              AMELIA
            Not with me around.
                    (to Samuel)
            What's your name, sweetie?

Samuel fidgets.

                            CHARLOTTE
            His name is Samuel.

                              AMELIA
            Hello, Samuel. Your Mother and I grew up
            together. I'm a couple years older, though.

He bashfully looks to Charlotte.

                              AMELIA
                    (to Charlotte)
            I'm not sure who you married.

                            CHARLOTTE
            Minister Dennis.

                              AMELIA
                    (blustered)
            Dennis? But. He's at least...

Amelia clocks Samuel watching her, and recomposes.

                              AMELIA
            I haven't heard his name in so long.

Charlotte's eyes widen as she focuses out the window.

Amelia follows Charlotte's eye line. Displeasure shades
her.

                              AMELIA
            She only gets gasoline. Never comes inside.
            I've seen her look in the windows, though. Word
            got out. The devils know I'm here.

WINDOW VIEW: A station attendant tends to Mildred's car.

INT./EXT. MILDRED'S CAR/DINER PARKING LOT - CONT.

With Ruth in the passenger seat, Mildred spots...

SIDE OF DINER: Charlotte's car parked.

Mildred suspiciously eyes the diner. Ruth notices.

                              RUTH
            What's wrong, Mother?

INT. DINER - CONT.

Amelia and Charlotte watch at the window. Charlotte grabs her umbrella.

> **CHARLOTTE**
> (takes Samuel's hand)
> We must go.

Charlotte pulls Samuel toward the exit.

> **AMELIA**
> You don't have to go because of her. You can stay, Charlotte.

Charlotte and Samuel exit.

Amelia watches out the window. Her hands anxious.

INT./EXT. MILDRED'S CAR/DINER PARKING LOT - CONT.

Mildred and Ruth's interest picks up as they watch...

Charlotte exit with Samuel. She raises her umbrella and takes his hand as they approach their car.

INT. DINER - CONT.

In cook's snap shirt and houndstooth pants, big BOBBY (40s), steps beside Amelia, who watches out the window.

> **BOBBY**
> Never saw one of them women supressionists come inside here.

Amelia nearly speaks. Doesn't. Watches Mildred's car.

> **BOBBY**
> She drove herself? I've only seen that older woman drive here to get fuel. Puts it on a tab. Her brother pays for it. At least, I heard it's her brother. Never know with those people.

> **AMELIA**
> The young one's married to the newer Minister. The other woman out there is married to the old minister.

> **BOBBY**
> Wonder if it's true about that guy in their town.

> **AMELIA**
> What guy?

15

                    BOBBY
There's a guy with. I don't know. His face is
an awful mess. I saw him walking, once.

                    AMELIA
Is what true?

                    BOBBY
I heard they tried to kill him because he did
something to little girls.

That kicks Amelia, but she calms.

                    AMELIA
He was driving that ruined bus sittin' over
there in the junk yard. When it crashed. That's
how his face got like that.

                    BOBBY
She just told you that?

As Nancy approaches, Amelia heads away.

                    NANCY
Bobby. You gonna cook up them orders? Customers
are waiting.

Bobby goes to the kitchen as Nancy looks out the window.

INT./EXT. MILDRED'S CAR (PARKED) - CONT.

Ruth uses a handkerchief to dab sweat from her forehead.

                    RUTH
Samuel got to go inside. Why can't--

                    MILDRED
--You will not go in there.

Mildred starts the engine.

Ruth pouts as Mildred shifts the car into drive.

INT. CHARLOTTE'S CAR (MOVING) - DINER DRIVEWAY - CONT.

As Charlotte slows the car, her eyes widen as she gazes
across the road to the...

VIEW OF JUNK YARD: Among ruined cars sits the old,
horribly damaged church bus, windows hauntingly gone.

                    SAMUEL (O.S.)
What happened to that bus?

CHARLOTTE: Stares out at the bus. Then, looks to the rearview mirror and her face drops. A car horn blares.

Samuel turns and looks out the back window.

MILDRED'S CAR

Ruth continues to pout as Mildred waits. Mildred lays on the obnoxiously loud horn.

INT./EXT. CHARLOTTE'S CAR (MOVING)/ROAD TO HAVEN - DAY

Nervous Samuel watches...

distressed Charlotte drive as she glances in the...

REARVIEW MIRROR: Mildred's car tailgates them.

> CHARLOTTE
> It fell off the mountain.

> SAMUEL
> How did a bus fall off a mountain?

> CHARLOTTE
> A car got in its way.

> SAMUEL
> Were there people in it?

> CHARLOTTE
> Yes.

> SAMUEL
> Did they get hurt?

> CHARLOTTE
> Two of them did... The other thirty-eight of
> them... went to heaven.

> SAMUEL
> Grandfather says heaven's really far away,
> where we can't see it.

Stressed, Charlotte pulls to the side of the road, near...

GABRIEL'S FARM PRODUCE STAND

Gabriel accepts money from a customer as Gabriel notices...

CHARLOTTE'S CAR

Samuel factors the situation as Charlotte sits distressed, her eyes on the side-view mirror.

Mildred's car pulls up alongside Charlotte. Mildred's gnawing eyes look to Charlotte.

> RUTH
> (pouts)
> Samuel got to go inside --

> MILDRED
> -- Shut up.

Charlotte nervously diverts her eyes.

FARM STAND

Mildred's car stops near the stand. She glares at...

Gabriel, who helps the customer.

> MILDRED
> (to Gabriel)
> Outcast! Sinner! You sinner!

As Mildred speeds away, the customer grabs the bag of produce and quickly heads to their car.

Charlotte exits her car and steps to the dirt gully on the side of the road. Bends over. Pukes.

Gabriel approaches and holds out a chunk of watermelon.

Charlotte shyly accepts it. She takes a big bite. As she chews, juice drips from her mouth.

> GABRIEL
> Did you visit Amelia?

Charlotte freezes, as if transfixed by an accusation.

> GABRIEL
> She works at the diner, you know?

Charlotte stiffhandedly drops the watermelon.

> GABRIEL
> Never seen you out of Haven. Does Minister
> Dennis know?

She gets in the car. Puts it in gear. Drives away.

He kicks the watermelon rind to the gully, and watches the car drive off.

INT. CHARLOTTE'S BEDROOM - DAWN

The ticking alarm clock on the dresser shows 5:59 A.M.

Dennis snores in his single bed.

On the other side of the veil curtain, her blankets pulled aside, Charlotte, in a bedgown, stares into insomnia, the baby bump evident. Dennis' snores continue.

ALARM CLOCK: The bells ring at 6:00 A.M. The hand of Dennis turns it off.

He continues to the bathroom in his full body underwear.

Charlotte opens her eyes to stare at the ceiling to the sound of Dennis pissing into the toilet.

BATHROOM - MINUTES LATER

The murky water of the tub splashes. Dennis is in the tub as he scrubs his face. He rinses the suds from his face.

>   **DENNIS**
>   (glumly)
>   I'm ready for my back.

Charlotte enters in her bedgown and messy hair. Sits on the tub, takes the washcloth. Unhappily scrubs his back.

She rushes to the toilet, kneels, and vomits.

>   **DENNIS**
>   How many more months do I have to listen to
>   this vileness?

She wipes her face. Nearly vomits. Gulps to stop it.

>   **CHARLOTTE**
>   Maybe five. Or, four. Months.

He throws the soap. It hits her head.

>   **DENNIS**
>   The favors you do for me. Come here.

She nearly stands from kneeling.

>   **DENNIS**
>   Crawl! CRAWL!

She crawls to the tub. He grasps hold of her hair and yanks her head back and forth as he laughs.

>   **DENNIS**
>   (lets go of her hair)
>   You disgust me. Now, get out.

She scampers and trips on her bed gown as she flees.

He deviously laughs. His smile dissolves and he stares.

INT. CHICKEN COOP - DAY

Eggs are gathered by crying Charlotte, hair a mess, in her bed gown. She places the eggs in a handled basket.

EXT. CHICKEN COOP/BACK YARD - DAY

Charlotte exits with the basket of eggs, removes some clothes from the drying line, then continues to the house.

INT. CARPENTRY - DAY

Wooden planks are sanded by men using hand tools.

A rather handsome young man wipes dust from a newly crafted church chair on a work table. He takes up a brush, and proceeds to oil-stain the wood.

From a distance, Dennis somewhat leeringly watches the handsome young man.

INT. KEATON DINING ROOM - EVENING

By candle light, Samuel eats with Grandfather.

An oil lantern is on the table near Dennis, as he eats and looks through paperwork. Near him sits Jeffrey.

> **JEFFREY**
> Twelve. The other church ordered twenty-seven pews, thirteen chairs, and a pedestal. No stain or varnish.

> **DENNIS**
> They should at least oil --

> **JEFFREY**
> -- They want them unfinished. That way, we can ship them before church camp.

Dennis impatiently shoves away the paperwork.

KITCHEN

As the window light fades, Charlotte lights a lantern. Then sits at the table with shy Betty as they eat dinner.

> **CHARLOTTE**
> Sometimes, I can feel him moving.

> **BETTY**
> Wouldn't you want the baby to be a girl?

Charlotte takes a deep breath and lets it out.

> **CHARLOTTE**
> That was a kick.

> **BETTY**
> Is there anything I can do?

Charlotte steadies her breath, reaches for her glass of milk, but jolts in pain. She spills the milk.

Betty rises and grabs a dishtowel.

> **HALLWAY**
> Dish towels are taken from the linen closet by Charlotte.

Betty, at the doorway, drops to her knees to wipe up milk that drips from Charlotte's dress.

> **CHARLOTTE**
> That's okay, Betty. You don't need --

Betty sees through the open door that...

BEDROOM: The curtain veil hangs in place between the single beds.

> **BETTY**
> (perplexed)
> But.

Charlotte pulls the door closed.

> **BETTY**
> You know you can take down the veil after your propagation.

Charlotte heads to the kitchen.

Betty remains perplexed.

KITCHEN

Charlotte wipes spilled milk from the table as Betty enters.

Charlotte puts the towel in the sink.

Betty sits, as if unsure.

Charlotte sits and continues to eat.

                         BETTY
                      (quietly)
          I'd like a baby.

                       CHARLOTTE
          They'll come along, in time.

                         BETTY
                    (as if to herself)
          We've been married seven years.

Silence settles in as Charlotte deflects her eyes. They
eat.

                         BETTY
          Do you miss your Mother? I mean, especially
          with Samuel, and a new --

                       CHARLOTTE
          -- Yes.

                       DENNIS (O.S.)
          We're finished.

DINING ROOM

The final potato slice is taken from his plate by Samuel
using his fingers. Grandfather watches him.

                        DENNIS
                      (sternly)
          With your fork, Samuel.

Charlotte enters and gathers the dirty dishes.

                        DENNIS
          Teach this boy manners.

Dennis notices...

Jeffrey watch Charlotte.

EXT. CHURCH - DAY

A mix of old cars and several dusty pickup trucks are
parked. Nearby, horses are hitched to covered carriages.

Other horses drink at the water trough beneath the oak
tree in the small corral.

INT. CHURCH - CONT.

The seven teenage girls sit in the front pew. Men are in
the middle pews. Women with children in the back pews.

Sincere-faced Allen sits among the men.

Next to Ruth, Mildred eyes the various church members.
Mildred's suspicions land on...

Charlotte, who sits with Samuel, subtly glances askance,
as if she can feel Mildred watch her.

PODIUM

Jeffrey sits in a chair as Dennis steps up to the lectern
and scans the congregation. Closes his eyes, as if to
receive revelatory messages. Then, opens his eyes.

> **DENNIS**
> (fervently)
> Banish ungodly deeds of the flesh to the
> cities, where the untrustworthy and the ruined
> souls of the lost rot in the stench of lust and
> sin.

Charlotte gains a frightful gaze as she listens.

Mildred continues to regard Charlotte.

> **DENNIS**
> (shouts)
> We are the righteous blessed. The confirmed.
> The hidden truth is our way.

Allen is absorbed by the sermon.

> **DENNIS**
> It is with humble heart that we bear this
> goodness by the sweat of our brows.

Worry traces Charlotte.

EXT. CHURCH - MINUTES LATER - DAY

Children exit into the bright sun, followed by women with
black umbrellas. No men. Mildred and Ruth raise umbrellas
as they exit.

INT. CHURCH - LATER - DAY

Allen's shut eyes as in prayer.

Dennis at the lectern observes in front of him...

The men kneel in a circle, heads bowed, eyes closed.

Dennis circles them. Stops near the handsome young man
from the carpentry, his eyes closed in prayer.

                    DENNIS
              (observes the handsome man)
        Know you are the righteous. Free from sin. Your
        innocence and purity will be rewarded in
        heaven.

Dennis continues to gaze at the handsome man.

INT. KEATON KITCHEN - NIGHT

Wood toy blocks are played with by Samuel on the floor.

                    SAMUEL
        Am I going to do that?

Charlotte cooks food as she towels sweat from her neck.

                    CHARLOTTE
        Do what?

                    SAMUEL
        Talk to people like Father does?

She turns to watch him play with the blocks.

                    CHARLOTTE
        You will be a good man.

His innocent eyes are contemplative as he looks to her.

She takes dinnerware from a drawer.

DINING ROOM - MOMENTS LATER

The tableware is set by tearful Charlotte.

She stops. Looks around, as if her thoughts collide. Her
breath shivers as she rubs her palms on her dress.

                    CHARLOTTE
              (quietly anguished)
        I must... There's got to be a way... There has
        got to be a way.

She contemplates and frustratedly huffs.

INT. CHURCH - NIGHT

Wall sconce candles flicker as men sit in the pews.

With his eyes closed, Dennis stands at the lectern.

                    DENNIS
                (his eyes open angrily)
        PERSEVERE AGAINST THE DECEPTION OF THE EVIL
        OUTSIDE FORCES!... They will steal your
        heavenly inheritance. The deceivers will
        mislead you to participate in their dreadful
        ways. The evil energy will saturate your soul.

Dennis again closes his eyes, as if to receive messages.
He opens his eyes and looks about, suspiciously.

                    DENNIS
        Keep your helpmate in line. On the narrow path.
        As a faithful wife. Rule over her.

Among the seated men, Allen appears eager.

                    DENNIS
        Those of you who are unmarried, your day of
        copulating with a blessed Daughter of Eve
        approaches. Remain obedient. The sacred journey
        of matrimony awaits you.

The men all rise.

                    THE MEN
        HENCEFORTH, EVIL! BE GONE!

Dennis watches the brethren with guarded satisfaction.

INT. DINER - DAY

A few truckers scarf down food together at a table.

At another table, Amelia, with a different pretty scarf
tied around her neck, gathers dirty dishes.

She glances out the side window, then quickly looks back
to it.

SIDE WINDOW: Beneath her umbrella stands Charlotte. She
steps out of sight, toward the back of the diner.

INT./EXT. CHARLOTTE'S CAR/BEHIND DINER - DAY

Sweat beads on his tender face as Samuel sits alone in the
car with windows down, he watches...

BESIDE BACK DOOR OF DINER

Amelia listens to Charlotte, who is shaded by her
umbrella. They speak in hushed tones.

                    CHARLOTTE
        I'm afraid.

                         AMELIA
          Of what?

                        CHARLOTTE
          Outside Forces.

                         AMELIA
               (the phrase hits her)
          I haven't heard that since... I left.

                        CHARLOTTE
          I have no one to confess to. I cannot speak
          such words to Minister Dennis.

                         AMELIA
          Confess what, Charlotte?

Charlotte checks over her shoulder.

Samuel watches from inside the car.

                        CHARLOTTE
               (whispers)
          The evil I've done.

                         AMELIA
          What did you do?

                        CHARLOTTE
          Not that Minister Dennis doesn't know. But I
          can't speak of it. I can't.

The back door of the diner opens. Nancy looks out.

                         NANCY
          Amelia. We have customers.

Nancy expectantly holds open the door.

                        CHARLOTTE
               (to Amelia)
          I must go.

Charlotte scampers away to the car.

Amelia and Nancy watch.

                         NANCY
          What was she telling you?

                         AMELIA
          Not sure. She whispers things.

Amelia, enters the door. Nancy curiously watches...

Charlotte's car pull to the driveway. Paused across from the junk yard with the twisted, dusty, windowless bus.

Nancy continues to watch. The car is heard driving away.

EXT. CARPENTRY LOADING DOCK - DAY

Dennis stands off to the side while...

Allen and a few other workers use clamps to unload logs from a flatbed truck.

Timothy exits the carpentry. He passes six men who carry the final log.

Timothy stops by Dennis and glances about, as if to check if anyone is near.

>   TIMOTHY
> If I stopped bringing logs, how would you
> survive?

Dennis stares ahead.

>   TIMOTHY
> I need an additional twenty-five dollars...
> Every truckload.

>   DENNIS
> Robbery.

Dennis glares at Timothy, who simply holds eye contact.

>   TIMOTHY
> You think any of your men are going to go into
> those mountains, and cut trees?... They might
> like being away from you.

>   DENNIS
> Sister Mildred would not approve of --

>   TIMOTHY
> -- She doesn't rule my life, as she does
> yours... I can sell the logs elsewhere.

Dennis diverts his eyes as Timothy waits.

>   DENNIS
> Starting next load.

>   TIMOTHY
> You will give me fifty more dollars for today.
> Twenty-five more after this.

A deal standoff. Then. Dennis slightly nods.

                              TIMOTHY
                    How could we be from the same womb?

Timothy heads toward and gets in the truck. Starts the
engine. Spins the tires in the gravel as he drives away.

EXT. HAVEN GENERAL STORE - DAY

Three children, in wrinkled, scuffed clothes exit,
followed by their Mother (mid-20s), in a long, wrinkled
dress. She raises her black umbrella to block the sun.

THE WOODEN WALKWAY

Timothy nods hello as he passes the woman, who frightfully
quickens her pace to follow her children.

INT. HAVEN GENERAL STORE - MINUTES LATER

Two Mothers (late teens - mid-20s), in drab, long dresses,
one with a baby, the other with children, shop among
shelves of basic groceries, simple clothing, and sparse,
basic home goods. They sneak glances at...

Timothy, who places his basket of goods on the counter
before a pious clerk, DAVID (40s).

                              DAVID
                    Will you be having any of the smoked meats
                    today, Brother Timothy?

                              TIMOTHY
                    I'm not your brother, David. Only two
                    unfortunate souls can call me that.

David waits as he suffers Timothy's impatience.

                              TIMOTHY
                    Unlike you, I hunt my own meat.

David proceeds to write down Timothy's purchases.

Ruth enters with Mildred. They notice Timothy.

Mildred appears displeased as she grabs a basket.

                              RUTH
                         (softly, to Mildred)
                    It's Uncle Timothy.

Mildred takes Ruth by the wrist and leads her to a
standard kitchen-cutlery shelf. Mildred selects a knife,
and considers the blade.

Timothy approaches with a lollipop.

Other Mothers sneak glances as they shop. Children watch.

> TIMOTHY
> (holds out the lollipop)
> It's nice to see you, Ruth. Would you like a
> lollipop?

Mildred grips the knife as she blocks Ruth.

> MILDRED
> You leave her alone.

> TIMOTHY
> Is an uncle not allowed to give his niece a
> lollipop?

Mildred notices the other Mothers watch. She steps aside
to watch Timothy continue to hold out the lollipop.

Ruth hesitates. Takes it.

> RUTH
> Thank you.

> TIMOTHY
> (to Mildred)
> Is there something you'd like to say?

Ignoring him, Mildred considers the kitchen supplies.

> TIMOTHY
> (to Ruth)
> One day you will be able to get out of this
> town, and meet your Mother.

Mildred marches over and smacks Timothy's face.

He's unmoved.

Ruth is stunned.

> TIMOTHY
> (to Mildred)
> Do you feel better, Mildred?

She steps away.

> TIMOTHY
> How's your husband?

Mildred steps back and smacks him again.

He seems humored.

MILDRED
Where's your wife and children? Everyone knows,
they left you.

TIMOTHY
Will you sleep better tonight?

Mildred steps away to shop. As if unconcerned.

The other Mothers pretend not to notice, as their children
watch...

Timothy return to the counter. David bags the purchases.

A girl watches, but is pulled away by her Mother.

TIMOTHY
(to anyone)
How do you think this town functions?

The Mother's eyes avoid him.

Children eye him.

Especially Ruth.

TIMOTHY
What would the carpentry do without logs?

Only ignored, as if he is not there.

TIMOTHY
How would your families survive not selling
furniture? Your farms are mostly barren... Why
don't you leave this place, like the others?
Those who didn't die.

Mothers ignore him as the children continue watching.

TIMOTHY
You treat me with abhorrence. Do my sins make
you feel worthy?

DAVID
Please, Brother Timothy.

TIMOTHY
I'm not your brother.

Timothy takes the shopping bag. Exits. The door slams.

RUTH
(quietly)
Mother, why did Uncle Timothy say that?

Mildred continues to shop.

> RUTH
>
> Mother?

> MILDRED
>
> He's none of your concern.

She glares at the other Mothers, who divert themselves.

Children eye Ruth, as she licks the lollipop.

EXT. GENERAL STORE - CONT. - DAY

Timothy looks at the sign on the door, "Henceforth, evil, be gone!" He unhooks it and flings it into the road.

He gets in the flatbed truck. Starts the engine. Drives.

Mildred exits the store with Ruth and her lollipop.

> MILDRED
>
> Sit down.

Ruth takes a seat as Mildred rushes off.

> RUTH
>
> Where are you going, Mother?

Mildred gets into the car. Starts the engine.

> RUTH
>
> Mother?

INT./EXT. TIMOTHY'S TRUCK (MOVING)/ROAD - DAY

As he touches his smacked cheek, Timothy drives toward the mountains. He looks to the rearview mirror.

> TIMOTHY
>
> The hell.

Mildred's car speeds up behind the truck, dangerously cuts in front of him, and slows as the truck nearly collides with the car. Both abruptly stop.

She storms from the car and to the truck.

> MILDRED
>
> Don't you ever say anything like that to her.

> TIMOTHY
>
> Or, what? Move your car.

She glares at him, turns, and heads back to the car.

He hops from the truck.

As she is about to enter the car, he grabs the back of her neck, and forces her to closely face him.

> TIMOTHY
> You don't own anyone!

He shoves her away. She nearly falls, catches her balance, turns back to him.

> TIMOTHY
> Mother left because of you. You made her miserable. I hope she's happy. Wherever she went.

She spits onto his chest.

> MILDRED
> It's clear why your wife left with your children. You're nothing.

She gets in the car, slams the door. Does a U-turn. Speeds back toward town.

He watches as his thoughts brew.

EXT. KEATON BACK PORCH - MOUSE CAGE - DAY

The mice eat bits of bread flicked into the cage by...

Samuel who calmly watches them.

INT. KEATON KITCHEN - DAY

A chunk of raw meat is chopped by a cleaver.

Charlotte takes bits of the meat and tosses them into a fry pan. She uses the cleaver to...

press onto the meat bits in the pan. Blood oozes from them and sizzles on the hot metal.

She dips her finger in, tastes it. Spits onto the floor.

She considers the cleaver. Feels its edge, then...

chops another chunk from the raw meat.

EXT. CHURCH MEMBER'S HOME - SMALL HORSE CORRAL - DAY

Dry oats are scooped into a horse feeder by, face unseen, the thin, raggedy man, Isaiah.

He pumps water into the trough as a couple of horses approach to drink.

EXT. CHURCH - DUSK

Lit candles are in the windows.

Several horses are tied to posts near dusty pickup trucks.

Timothy's truck rumbles up. The engine cuts. He gets out.

He steps to the front of the truck. Rests against it. Nearly smiles. It fades. He looks up to...

the steeple, where a raven is perched. Watching.

INT. CHURCH PARLOR ROOM - NIGHT

A wooden sign, "Henceforth, evil, be gone!" on the office door at the end of the room lit by wall candle sconces.

Along the walls in chairs sit eight slender men (40s to 50s), chopped hair, dusty slacks, rumpled white shirts.

The office door opens. Jeffrey steps into the parlor. Points to...

sincere-faced Allen, who dutifully rises.

OFFICE

Dennis sits at the lamp-lit desk.

Allen enters and studiously sits in a chair.

> **DENNIS**
> Do you have sins to confess?

> **ALLEN**
> I have been steadfast and obedient.

Dennis winces. He closes his eyes, as if to receive prophecy. Opens his eyes. Stares at Allen.

> **ALLEN**
> What is it, Minister Dennis?

Dennis continues to stare at him.

PARLOR

Jeffrey stands as the other men remain seated.

The outside door opens. Timothy enters and glances about.

The men deflect their eyes as Timothy sits in a chair.

> **TIMOTHY**
> (to anyone)
> Are you being steadfast?

Few men dare to eye him.

> **TIMOTHY**
> Are you refraining from evil?... Are you
> taunted by the vile Outside Forces?

> **JEFFREY**
> Brother Timothy. You --

> **TIMOTHY**
> -- Why do you have no children, Jeffrey?... Is
> your wife barren? Is your heart impure?

Jeffrey's face blazes red.

> **TIMOTHY**
> The sins you focus on in others... Why are
> those sins at the forefront of your thoughts?

Men stare forward. Some askance glance at Timothy.

> **TIMOTHY**
> (to anyone)
> Do you think I'm evil?... About that narrow
> path to the blessings you teach of: What are
> those blessings, exactly?

A man glares at him.

> **TIMOTHY**
> (to the man)
> Who are you to judge me? Where would you be
> without me? What would you do?

All eyes look at him.

> **TIMOTHY**
> And, we wait... To speak with the great leader.

OFFICE

Dennis pitifully listens.

> **ALLEN**
> (nearly in tears)
> My home is in order. A new veil is hung in the
> bedroom. I have burned the old veil, as you had
> instructed. I am ready for a wife.

34

DENNIS

The obedient are rewarded in heaven. There are only seven. Your brethren also have been obediently waiting.

ALLEN

I've waited years for my Daughter of Eve. I must have one! You said, since my wife and child were killed, I'd be rewarded --

DENNIS

-- There will be new brides ready in a few years... Perhaps, my niece. Ruth.

ALLEN

Why not one of the younger men? I'm forty-nine. You're giving younger --

DENNIS

-- I have prayed on this. Are you telling me you doubt holy revelation?

Conflicted with the challenge, Allen's forehead creases.

DENNIS

You are to endure in faith. In obedience. The brethren will honor your sacrifice, Brother Allen.

Allen nearly shakes his head, no. Then, hesitantly nods.

ALLEN
(stands)
Thy will be done.

Allen turns. Pauses. Nearly speaks. Exits. Door shuts.

Dennis sits back and reflects. Cynically snickers.

PARLOR

Allen mopes from the office and through the room as the brethren watch. Allen stops as he notices Timothy.

ALLEN

You? By what do you deserve such reward?

Timothy seems unsure as Allen speedily exits to the outside. The door slams.

DENNIS (O.S.)
(loudly)
Next! Enter, and sin no more!

OFFICE

Timothy enters. Kicks the door shut.

Dennis practically shivers in displeasure.

Timothy kicks the chair aside and kneels before the desk.

>   TIMOTHY
> I must confess to the worthy one.

>   DENNIS
> You --

>   TIMOTHY
> -- As you know, I have done again the same as
> what I had done years prior. But with a
> willingness of each of us.

Dennis is livid.

>   TIMOTHY
> The evil pleasure. Does it bother you?
>   (cynically smirks)
> Do my deeds please you? Do they provide you
> status in the community you deceive?

Dennis broils.

>   TIMOTHY
> My wife has left me. Took the children
> someplace I don't know. Who shall I turn to for
> my needs?

PARLOR

The brethren wait. Some exchange poker-faced glances.

>   TIMOTHY (O.S.)
>   (loudly)
> I'm not sorry!

OFFICE

Dennis stands from the chair.

>   DENNIS
>   (quietly)
> Get out.

He watches as...

Timothy takes hold of the fallen chair. Places it in front
of the desk. Sits.

                    TIMOTHY
Am I to confess to your sins? Am I to go to
your imaginary hell, and suffer your damnation?
By your rules? Or, perhaps, our darling
sister's rules?

                    DENNIS
              (shouts)
HENCEFORTH, EVIL, BE GONE!

              MEN IN OTHER ROOM (O.S.)
HENCEFORTH, EVIL, BE GONE!

                    TIMOTHY
Why do you remain here? What do you get
out of being Mildred's puppet? Why do you
not seek your own satisfaction?

He mockingly laughs as he stands.

                    TIMOTHY
Living to please others. As if they matter. You
are a fool.

Dennis glares.

PARLOR

Timothy steps from the office and leaves the door ajar.

The men watch, as...

Timothy stops, as if he is to speak. His gaze lacerates a
few of them as they wilt.

Timothy exits.

                    DENNIS (O.S.)
Next. Enter, and sin no more.

Jeffrey points to a man, who dutifully stands.

CHAPEL - LATER - NIGHT

Dennis' eyes closed. Sweat streaks his face. Red-faced, he
stands before the lectern. His closed eyes open wide.

                    DENNIS
              (pleads fervently)
You do not know how evil they are. We are
protected from the Outside Forces. Those of the
corrupt cities. Painted ladies. Whores! Men
alone and their sinful dancing. Doing
abhorrent, ghastly acts. THEY ARE LIONS! THEY
WILL EAT YOU ALIVE!

Sweat soaks his shirt. He puts forth his hands, as if to offer himself while he works to catch his breath.

>   DENNIS
>   Do you not understand my life mission?

He grasps his chest.

>   DENNIS
>   (squeals as he hollers)
>   HENCEFORTH, EVIL, BE GONE!

He steps around the lectern. Falls to his knees. Cries.

Lowers his forehead to the floor. He has preached to...

the chapel of empty pews.

The door opens, Jeffrey enters and runs to...

Crying Dennis, forehead on the floor.

Jeffrey kneels and holds Dennis.

>   DENNIS
>   Can't they see I am here to protect them from
>   themselves? They will sin!

Jeffrey continues to hold him as he cries.

INT. KEATON DINING ROOM - NIGHT

By candlelight, Samuel and Grandfather eat dinner.

KITCHEN

Charlotte wearily eats alone. She hears commotion from the...

DINING ROOM

Samuel and Grandfather watch as...

Dennis, a sweaty mess, enters from the living room. He sits, and closes his eyes.

>   SAMUEL
>   Father, we said grace.

Dennis looks to Samuel.

>   GRANDFATHER
>   Eat your dinner, Minister.

Dennis tiredly considers him.

                    DENNIS
          Why did Mother leave you?... Where did she
          go?... What is she doing?

Grandfather simply eats.

                    DENNIS
          Now Timothy's wife is gone.

Charlotte enters with a plate of food she places before
Dennis. He watches as she returns to the kitchen.

Dennis stares at the food. Finally, he picks up a fork.
Jabs it into a chunk of meat. Eats.

INT. ALLEN'S LIVING ROOM - NIGHT

Wall sconce candles light the tidy room furnished with
plain wooden furniture.

Allen stands at the doorway. He sadly looks around the
room, as if all hope is lost.

BEDROOM

A veil curtain hangs between the two single beds.

Allen stops in the doorway. Calmly looks at the veil.

KITCHEN - LATER

A candle flickers on the table beside a shotgun with a box
of rounds next to it. The table is set for two.

Seated at the table, Allen stares.

EXT. KEATON BACKYARD/ORCHARD - DAY

Dennis approaches the dusty old pickup truck.

Among the apple trees, sweaty Charlotte in a long, dusty
dress picks fruit. Places them in...

a basket held by Samuel.

Dennis gets into the pickup truck. Starts the engine.

Charlotte continues to harvest. She finally turns.

The truck drives away down the road.

Charlotte pauses as the sound of the truck fades. She
wipes sweat from her face, takes the basket from Samuel,
who follows her toward the house.

EXT. BRUSHY WILDLAND HILLSIDE - DAY

A gravel road ends in the distance, where a car is parked beside a white picket-fenced area. Two people stand, one with an umbrella. They are in a...

GRAVEYARD

A raven rests on a simple, upright gravestone listing:
      "To Heaven August 1, 1950
      Thomas Bowers, age 33
      Bridget Bowers, age 32
      Jeremiah Bowers, age 12
      Luke Bowers, age 10"

Shaded by her umbrella, with her hand on her pregnant belly, Charlotte gazes at...

the raven.

Samuel inches forward.

The raven flies away.

Samuel watches it fly, then he curiously looks at...

the other, sun scorched headstones.

Charlotte remains focused on the Bowers gravestone.

> **SAMUEL**
> Why are you looking at that one?

> **CHARLOTTE**
> It has the names of my parents and brothers.

> **SAMUEL**
> Where are they?

> **CHARLOTTE**
> Heaven.

> **SAMUEL**
> Like the people on the bus?

> **CHARLOTTE**
> Yes... They were on the bus.

She looks over...

the names on other gravestones with similar dates listed.

Samuel wanders outside the picket fence, and tosses a stone toward the distant town.

Charlotte approaches the car, folds her umbrella, gestures for Samuel.

She gets in the car, as does he. The engine starts.

Two ravens fly about.

One lands on the picket fence.

The other on a gravestone.

INT. DINER - DAY

At a table, a trucker eats as he curiously watches...

Charlotte and Samuel, at a window table. Samuel sips from a glass of ice water. Charlotte factors as...

Truckers settle at a different table as Amelia, another pretty scarf around her neck, takes their orders.

Nancy stands with an order pad in hand at Charlotte's table.

> **NANCY**
> Nothing? Well, what about a milkshake?
> (to Samuel)
> You'd like a milkshake, wouldn't you, sonny?

Samuel shyly looks to Charlotte.

> **CHARLOTTE**
> I'm sorry.

Charlotte stands, grabs her umbrella, takes Samuel's hand, and leads him out the door.

Nancy watches, as if pleased.

Amelia rushes over. Nancy nearly blocks her.

> **NANCY**
> Amelia, we can't keep letting them --

> **AMELIA**
> -- She needs a friend.

Nancy again blocks her.

> **AMELIA**
> How dare you.

> **NANCY**
> You're wasting your time. She's married, isn't she?

                    AMELIA
          How did your marriage work out?

Nancy sneers.

COOK'S WINDOW: Bobby slides plates of food onto the shelf
as he looks out to the diner. He taps the bell.

Nancy listens to Amelia.

                    AMELIA
          She's not bothering anyone here. There's empty
          tables.

Amelia removes a cash tip and dirty dishes from a table.

                    NANCY
          Why do you care about those people? They're
          backwards. If they want out, they should leave.
          Most already have. At least, the ones who had
          sense. Or didn't die.

Amelia nearly speaks. Holds off. Heads to the cook's
window.

Nancy takes the remaining water glasses from the table and
turns to see...

Amelia carry plates of food to the truckers. She sweetly
smiles as she gives them their food.

Nancy watches...

One trucker puts a hand on Amelia's waist. She playfully
slaps away his hand. The others haw at his expense.

Nancy continues to observe.

INT./EXT. CHARLOTTE'S CAR (MOVING)/LITTLE OLD HOUSE - DAY

With Samuel in the passenger seat, Charlotte slows to a
stop as she looks out to...

A distant, shabby, whitewashed house, where, his face not
seen, Isaiah uses a metal bucket to water his sparse
vegetable garden next to a small orchard.

                    SAMUEL (O.S.)
          Why is he always alone?

Charlotte pulls away, drives down the road.

                    SAMUEL
          Where's his family?

> **CHARLOTTE**
> They went away.

> **SAMUEL**
> To heaven?

> **CHARLOTTE**
> No. To another house.

Charlotte stares as she drives.

ISAIAH

His face remains unseen, he faces the other way as he watches the car.

INT. CHARLOTTE'S KITCHEN - DAY

At the open window with a view of the orchard and the mountains beyond, Charlotte sits on the sill with one hand on her baby bump. As her other hand uses a pie tin to fan her sweaty face.

> **DENNIS** (O.S.)
> (irritable)
> Are there more potatoes?

Charlotte stares out the window.

The door opens. Dennis enters.

Charlotte frightfully backs against the wall.

> **DENNIS**
> (gets in her face)
> Woman. Do you spite me?

He backhands her upside her head.

Dizzily, she balances herself on the counter.

He grabs her hair and shakes her head.

> **DENNIS**
> (shoves her toward stove)
> I want more potatoes.

She grabs a towel and picks up the pot from the stove.

DINING ROOM

Samuel and Grandfather eat.

Irritated Dennis angrily returns to the table.

Sweaty Charlotte scoops mashed potatoes from the pot and spoons it onto Dennis' plate.

>   **DENNIS**
>   (smacks the table)
>   Get back to the kitchen.

She exits.

Dennis suspiciously considers the kitchen door as he pours gravy onto his plate of mashed potatoes.

KITCHEN - LATER

The light from the window fades as Charlotte rinses her face at the sink. As it drips, she eyes the meat cleaver on the counter. Contemplatively, she feels its blade.

EXT. KEATON BACKYARD - DUSK

The intense tangerine sun sets over the mountains.

The meat cleaver in her hand, Charlotte's face drips as she is mesmerized by the brilliant sunset.

INT. CHARLOTTE'S BEDROOM - NIGHT

Dennis snores on his side of the veil. The clock ticks.

With the meat cleaver in hand, Charlotte stands on her side of the veil.

Dennis continues to snore. The veil slightly moves.

CHARLOTTE'S SIDE

She raises the cleaver as she grasps part of the veil. His snores stop. She retreats.

ALARM CLOCK: Hands strike 6 A.M. The bells clang.

Charlotte lies down and slides the cleaver beneath the blanket. Closes her eyes. The alarm stops.

Dennis steps up to her bed in his full-length underwear.

The handle of the cleaver sticks out from the blanket.

He grabs the cleaver and throws it against the wall.

Her eyes pop open. His hand forcefully presses on her upper chest. Her breath presses out.

His face gets too close.

                         DENNIS
                    (evilly whispers)
          Do you want to suffer the eternal flames of
          hell?

She fearfully shakes her head. He presses harder.

                       CHARLOTTE
                    (struggles to breathe)
          I'm with child.

                         DENNIS
          What would your filthy children do without me?
          Who would take you in? You're a tainted woman.

He removes his hand. She finally breathes.

                         DENNIS
          Make me breakfast.

The bathroom door slams. He is heard pissing.

Dazed and out of breath, Charlotte sits up.

INT. CARPENTRY - DAY

Various workers sand chairs. They stop to see...

Charlotte close her umbrella as she makes her way through
the carpentry. Samuel tags along.

The carpenters return to their work.

CARPENTRY OFFICE

Dennis makes notes in a ledger as Jeffrey stands near.

                         DENNIS
          Order the drill bits, and five new sander
          belts. Twenty gallons of varnish.

Jeffrey writes notes.

LOBBY

Charlotte and Samuel enter and take seats, and look to
the...

OFFICE WINDOWS

Dennis looks through the paperwork on his desk as Jeffrey
notices Charlotte.

Dennis looks up to the window. Anger crosses his face.

LOBBY

Charlotte and Samuel cower as Dennis stands over them.

>   CHARLOTTE
>   It's not so hot in here.

>   DENNIS
>   Go home. Open the windows.

>   CHARLOTTE
>   I feel faint. I feel --

>   DENNIS
>   -- A woman does not belong here.

>   CHARLOTTE
>   Mildred is here all the time.

He gestures as if to backhand her. She tilts away as he snivels.

>   DENNIS
>   (lowers his hand)
>   You talk to me so. After all I do for you. You
>   had no family. I took you in.

>   SAMUEL
>   It's hot, Father.

Dennis glares at Samuel, who defiantly eyes him.

Charlotte grabs Samuel's hand and pulls him from the room.

EXT. CARPENTRY - MOMENTS LATER - DAY

Shaded by her umbrella, Charlotte leads Samuel through the scorched dirt parking lot. Dust rises with each step.

At the loading dock, workers unload the flatbed truck of logs. Among them is Timothy. He stops to watch...

Charlotte, who takes Samuel's hand and goes faster while Samuel looks back toward...

Timothy, who continues to watch.

The men unloading logs cautiously glance at Timothy and Charlotte.

EXT. HAVEN GENERAL STORE/CHARLOTTE'S CAR - DAY

Charlotte exits with a grocery bag. Samuel follows her.

She places the bag in the car as Samuel gets in.

SIDE OF STORE

Face unseen, Isaiah sits in the shade, his back against the wall.

CHARLOTTE'S CAR

Samuel sits in the passenger seat as his concerned eyes watch...

SIDE OF STORE

Charlotte holds out a loaf of bread to Isaiah.

He looks up. His face is badly scarred and jaw twisted. He babbles indecipherably.

She hesitantly places the loaf of bread down beside him.

He again babbles.

>   CHARLOTTE
>   I'm sorry. I don't understand.

He scratches a finger into the...

DRY SOIL: The words: "She is not hers."

Charlotte considers it, but shakes her head.

>   CHARLOTTE
>   I don't know how to read.

He points to the words and mumbles.

Charlotte forgivingly bows and returns to the car.

Isaiah stares at the words he scratched in the soil.

CHARLOTTE'S CAR

Disturbed, Charlotte gets in.

>   SAMUEL
>   Did he talk? He can't talk.

She puts the car into gear, and drives.

>   CHARLOTTE
>   Don't mention to Minister Dennis that we saw
>   the man.

Samuel ponders that.

INT. CHURCH - NIGHT

In candlelight, a circle of a dozen men kneel, heads bowed, eyes closed, arms folded, in silent prayer. They include...

the handsome young man from the carpentry.

Also among them, Allen's sad eyes open as he contemplates the floor.

Dennis stands before the lectern.

> **DENNIS**
> The season will soon be for the wedding. We are to replenish Haven with young hearts to raise into our righteousness.

Jeffrey opens his eyes to notice...

Allen's sad stare at the floor.

> **DENNIS** (O.S.)
> The long-suffering, obedient, and strong in the faith will enjoy the rewards of endless blessings. For eternity.

Allen notices Jeffrey watching and closes his eyes.

> **DENNIS**
> We will all live in the glory of heaven.

Jeffrey sees that...

Dennis gazes, even lustfully, over the handsome young man whose eyes remain closed.

EXT. DINER - DAY

A couple of young women road trippers in shorts and sandals exit the diner, followed by a young man, also in shorts. They pass the contrast of...

Charlotte shaded by her umbrella. Samuel beside her.

Charlotte draws down the umbrella as they watch the trio.

> **YOUNG MAN**
> (cynically to friends)
> What century are we in?

As the trio continues, one of the girls smacks him on the arm to hush as the other girl giggles.

Charlotte and Samuel watch.

                    SAMUEL
              (RE: the shorts)
    What happened to their pants, Mother?

The trio hops into a convertible car.

                    SAMUEL
              (perplexed)
    That car doesn't have a top.

The road trippers start the engine and turn up the radio
to 50s rock-n-roll.

Samuel and Charlotte watch the car speed away.

INT. DINER - DAY

Several truckers hungrily eat at the large table.

WINDOW BOOTH

Amelia sits in her waitress uniform, another pretty scarf
around her neck. She pours catsup onto French fries for
Samuel as he sits across from her, next to Charlotte.

                    AMELIA
    ... The city is very, very different. There are
    many cars. And stores, houses, and buildings,
    and people dressed all sorts of ways.

                    CHARLOTTE
    Isn't the city filled with sinners?

Charlotte waits, as Amelia gathers thoughts.

                    AMELIA
    It's probably not what you would expect. Most
    people are friendly. Most don't seem to notice
    each other. They're busy with their own lives.

Charlotte takes that in.

                    AMELIA
    Whatever happened to Betty?

                    CHARLOTTE
    She married Brother Jeffrey.

                    AMELIA
    I thought he left... Moved to Oregon, or some
    place.

                    CHARLOTTE
    Where is that?

Amelia is hit by the innocence.

> **AMELIA**
> It's a place up north. About a day's drive.

Amelia notices...

ACROSS THE DINER: Nancy sets a table. Beyond her, at the cook's window, Bobby is busy at the grill, his helper, Lewis with him.

WINDOW BOOTH

Amelia offers Charlotte a blink of a smile.

> **AMELIA**
> You've never. You've never, ever left Haven?

> **CHARLOTTE**
> I've been to church camp. Up in the mountain.

> **AMELIA**
> I mean. Somewhere like... San Francisco.

> **CHARLOTTE**
> I've heard of it. Is it a city?

As if baffled. Amelia reconfigures.

> **AMELIA**
> I was living in Los Angeles... It's a city. Six
> hours drive south... I got into trouble
> there... They put me in the pen.

Charlotte clearly doesn't understand.

> **AMELIA**
> The penitentiary... I was in prison.

Charlotte waits.

> **AMELIA**
> The police arrested me. For spending time with
> certain men.

Charlotte obviously doesn't understand.

> **AMELIA**
> When some men are away from their wives,
> they'll pay money... to be close to a woman.

Amelia considers Samuel, as he eats French fries.

                              AMELIA
                    (to Charlotte)
          I was in prison for four years. They let me out
          six months ago... I can't live in Los Angeles.
          One man was a wealthy politician. I was in the
          newspapers. It made him angry. And, I got...

Charlotte contemplates her innocent gaze.

                              AMELIA
          Newspapers are... They're like... A book, sort
          of. But not... Never mind... I'll tell you
          another time.

Charlotte takes a napkin and wipes Samuel's fingers.

Amelia watches as her face traces with realization.

INT./EXT. MILDRED'S CAR/DINER PARKING LOT - CONT.

Bored, Ruth waits in the car.

Mildred stands nearby, her suspicious eyes watch the...

DINER WINDOWS: Charlotte, Samuel, and Amelia can be seen
as they sit inside at the window table.

INT. DINER - CONT.

The eating truckers pause to watch as...

Mildred abruptly steps up to where Amelia, Charlotte, and
Samuel sit.

                              MILDRED
                    (demands Charlotte)
          Leave this place.

Charlotte pops up as Amelia stands.

                              AMELIA
                    (to Mildred)
          You leave her alone.

                              MILDRED
          How dare you address me.

                              AMELIA
          Get the hell out of here.

Charlotte grabs her umbrella and Samuel's hand as she
heads for the exit.

                    AMELIA
          Charlotte. Don't leave. You don't need to
          listen to her.

Charlotte and Samuel exit.

The truckers watch the spectacle.

                    MILDRED
                (to Amelia)
          You are an outcast. You are a sinner.

                    AMELIA
          Get out.

Mildred looks about the place.

Truckers eye her.

She storms out.

Bobby approaches Amelia.

                    BOBBY
          What'd she say to you?

Amelia and Bobby notice Nancy approach.

                    NANCY
          Amelia, you can't speak that way to the
          customers.

                    AMELIA
          What's that bitter woman gonna do? Drive
          twenty-seven-miles down the road to the next
          gas station?

                    NANCY
          Amelia.

                    AMELIA
          That bitch talks to Charlotte as if she owns
          her.

                    NANCY
          You watch your mouth.

Amelia grabs the dirty dishes from the table.

                    AMELIA
                (walks away)
          These truckers have heard worse.

                    NANCY
               (bitterly, to Bobby)
          Some people think they can solve everyone's
          problems. They can't even solve their own.

Bobby shrugs and returns to the kitchen as Nancy watches
out the window.

INT./EXT CHARLOTTE'S CAR (MOVING)/ROAD TOWARD HAVEN - DAY

Charlotte drives with Samuel in the passenger seat. She
glances in the...

REARVIEW MIRROR: Mildred's car tailgates them.

Charlotte tenses as she drives.

Samuel turns to see out the...

BACK WINDOW: Mildred's car continues to tailgates.

EXT. HILLTOP - DAY - CONT.

A distant, high view of the highway, gas station, diner,
and the mountain pass road, where Mildred's car tailgates
Charlotte's.

Isaiah sits on a horse as he watches the cars below.

INT. KEATON DINING ROOM - NIGHT

Sweaty Dennis lividly glares.

                    DENNIS
          You are never to drive outside of Haven. Ever!

Sweaty Charlotte serves food to Samuel and
Grandfather.

She uses her sleeve to wipe sweat from her face.

                  CHARLOTTE
               (shyly)
          It's difficult being pregnant in this heat.

                    DENNIS
          Your words are vulgar.

                  CHARLOTTE
          With child. Please, excuse.

Charlotte flees to the kitchen.

Dennis' glare lingers on the door.

53

> GRANDFATHER
> Should we say the blessing?

KITCHEN

A glass of water and plate of uneaten food are...

Stared at by sweating Charlotte.

She lifts the glass of water and pours it over her head. A deep breath. Water drips from her as she thinks.

INT. CHURCH - DAY

Sweating, Dennis and Jeffrey are in the seats near the podium.

The scattering of congregants sits attentively.

The sweating seven teenage girls are in the front pew.

Men in the rows behind them, their faces streaked with sweat.

Also sweating, women and children in the back rows.

Sorrowful and sweaty, Allen sits alone, his eyes tiredly drift to the teenage girls.

Among the women, Mildred sternly stands from her pew.

> MILDRED
> The state of Charlotte Keaton. I confronted her at the truck station diner, conversing with a known outcast.

Wiping her sweaty face, Charlotte slowly stands and is subjected to stares of shame.

> CHARLOTTE
> I was there to show my boy the trucks. I went inside. They have cold air. I am tender in health. It's been so hot --

> MILDRED
> -- Amelia is a harlot!

People gasp. Some whisper to each other.

Mildred eyes them.

They silence.

> CHARLOTTE
> I didn't know it was her.

MILDRED
You have revisited her.

CHARLOTTE
I was being nice. She gave us water.

MILDRED
She is an outcast. A sinner.

CHARLOTTE
I didn't know it was her. I didn't know.

Other women gasp.

Ruth curiously looks about, as if slightly entertained.

Mildred glares at Ruth, and gestures as if ready to hit her.

Ruth flinches and leans away.

MILDRED
(points to Charlotte)
She is a sinner! Shame!

OTHER WOMEN
(chant to Charlotte)
Shame! Shame! Shame! Shame! Shame!

CHARLOTTE
I didn't know it was her!

CHURCH MEETING ROOM - LATER - DAY

Stern and sweaty Mildred stands watch.

In 12 chairs are 12 men in wrinkled white shirts. Their faces shimmer with sweat.

Including Dennis and Jeffrey.

Against an opposite wall stands sweat-drenched Charlotte.

CHARLOTTE
I felt ill. I went in for the cold air... They have a machine that makes cold air.

DENNIS
We have been given the air from God. We do not alter the air.

CHARLOTTE
You do not know what it's like to be with child.

MILDRED

You spoke with someone of the Outside Forces.
You lie, and you shame the community.

CHARLOTTE

She was nice.

DENNIS

Amelia is not among us. Your calling is to
raise your children in the flock.

CHARLOTTE

I am a good Mother. I am good!

DENNIS

You will not go to church camp. You are to stay
in Haven. You will not have access to the car.
You will repent of your sins.

Mildred smirks as if delighted.

DENNIS

Go home and attend to your child!

Charlotte shamefully bows her head as she exits.

DENNIS
(to Mildred)
The rest of the meeting will be amongst the
brethren.

The men wait.

Mildred eyes them. Huffs. Exits.

INT. CHARLOTTE'S BEDROOM - NIGHT

The alarm clock ticks as Dennis' snores are heard.

On her half of the room, divided by the veil, sweaty
Charlotte in bed. No blankets, but in her full bed gown.
Her hands rest on her baby bump.

CHARLOTTE
(softly)
What if...

Dennis' snores stop as he rolls to his side.

Charlotte closes her eyes. Sweat streaks her face.

The clock ticks. Tick. Tick. Tick. Tick.

Dennis again snores.

Charlotte's eyes open as if she has had a realization.
Tick. Tick. Tick. Tick. Tick.

EXT. KEATON BARN - DAY

Samuel is on a horse as he holds on tightly.

Charlotte struggles on a stool with her skirt gathered to
her thighs as she gets onto the saddle in front of him.

Samuel raises the umbrella to shade them.

She guides the horse toward a trail into the hills.

EXT. DINER PARKING LOT - DAY

A friendly TRUCKER (40s), approaches near where...

Under the umbrella, Charlotte sweats as she watches...

Samuel admires a large hauling truck.

>   **TRUCKER**
>   (to Samuel)
>   Like the truck, do you?

Charlotte and Samuel turn to see him. He opens the door.

>   **TRUCKER**
>   Wanna see the cabin?

Samuel turns to Charlotte, who slightly nods approval.

Samuel cautiously steps over and looks into the truck.

>   **TRUCKER**
>   Go ahead, little fella. You can climb up, if
>   you want.

Eyes full of wonder, Samuel climbs up and in, to sit
before the steering wheel.

>   **CHARLOTTE**
>   That's enough now. Don't want to keep you from
>   your job.

>   **TRUCKER**
>   It's okay. I'm stayin' here 'til the sun tilts.
>   Too hot to be driving.

Samuel climbs down from the truck and trots over to...

Charlotte, who takes his hand.

The Trucker seems unsure as he watches...

Charlotte lead Samuel away toward the diner.

INT. DINER - CONT.

Nancy takes orders from a few truckers at a table.

DOOR: Charlotte enters with Samuel as she lowers her umbrella. They slide into seats at a window booth.

Amelia, a pretty scarf around her neck, places food on a table where a trucker sits alone. She winks and leaves.

He watches her appreciatively as he picks up the fork.

MINUTES LATER

Amelia joins Charlotte at the booth, where Samuel eats a burger.

Amelia considers Charlotte's baby bump.

> **AMELIA**
> I remember this heat when I was pregnant. Wish I had air conditioning back then.

> **CHARLOTTE**
> (baffled)
> You have a child?

> **AMELIA**
> I thought everyone knew.

Amelia checks over her shoulder.

The seated truckers eat and talk as Nancy works at the cash register.

Amelia turns back to Charlotte.

> **AMELIA**
> I had a baby when I was fourteen.

> **CHARLOTTE**
> But... you weren't married. Who --

Charlotte stops, as if to avoid being intrusive.

> **AMELIA**
> The Campbell boy. He told his parents when we realized.

Amelia stops as she notices...

Samuel's innocent eyes watch as he eats.

CHARLOTTE

The Campbell boy. He's been gone.

AMELIA

His Mother said she didn't want to be related to Mother. So, they moved away.

Amelia waits as Charlotte appears to reflect on the news.

AMELIA

I heard he died in... Korea.

CHARLOTTE
(saddens)
The boys who went to that war... None of them returned. Not a single one.

AMELIA

At least, not to Haven. After seeing the real world. They didn't all die.

Charlotte takes a napkin to wipe Samuel's face.

AMELIA

Mother kept me in the house. For months. She padded her belly beneath her dress, with a folded towel. No matter how hot it got that summer.

Amelia checks Samuel, who plays with an ice cube.

AMELIA
(to Charlotte)
Father forced me into his car. He drove to the chapel and shoved me in the bus... Uncle Dennis was to drive. But he had stepped out. And Father simply drove it away. With everyone on it. All of those poor people.

Amelia stares out of the...

DINER WINDOW: Across the street sits the junk yard dominated by the mangled, windowless bus.

CHARLOTTE

I went into the church to use the bathroom. I came out, and the bus was gone. Your mother was yelling at Minister Dennis. She got into your father's car, and sped away.

AMELIA
(surprised)
I thought you were on the bus, and you survived.

                    CHARLOTTE
My parents and my three brothers were.

                    AMELIA
I can't imagine what you've been through.

                    CHARLOTTE
The Reynold's family took me in. But then, they
moved away. Like many of the other families. I
was thirteen. Then Minister Dennis.

                    AMELIA
Married you.

                    CHARLOTTE
I was fourteen, by then.

Amelia disgusted, her gaze lands out the window.

                    AMELIA
You'd think they'd get rid of that bus after
all these years.

                    CHARLOTTE
Where's your baby?

Amelia studies Charlotte.

                    AMELIA
Mother took her.

                    CHARLOTTE
        (startled)
Ruth?

                    AMELIA
She wanted a boy — so he could inherit the
church. I didn't deliver that. The baby would
have been too young, anyway. With Father
injured so badly, she chose Uncle Dennis.

Impatiently, Nancy approaches.

                    NANCY
Amelia, your customers need their bill.

Amelia taps Charlotte's hand. Gets up and heads off to the
customers.

Nancy follows her.

Charlotte sits confounded.

                    SAMUEL
What does died mean?

Charlotte's eyes worry.

> CHARLOTTE
> I'm not sure.

EXT. BACK DOOR OF DINER - MINUTES LATER - DAY

Bobby dumps a trash bucket into the waste bin. Curiosity
draws his face as he sees...

BY THE SHADE TREE: Charlotte gets onto the horse with
Samuel, who raises the umbrella.

Charlotte guides the horse into the brushland toward the
hills.

INT. DINER - COOK'S WINDOW - MOMENTS LATER - DAY

Amelia hands Bobby an order.

> BOBBY
> That friend of yours rode a horse here.

> AMELIA
> A horse? She has a car.

> BOBBY
> I guess it's shorter over the hills. They don't
> have to take the mountain pass.

EXT. DINER BACK DOOR - MOMENTS LATER - DAY

Amelia exits and scans the hills.

THE HILL CREST: On the horse, Charlotte with Samuel
holding up the umbrella to shade them. They ride over the
crest.

Amelia watches.

INT. CARPENTRY - DAY

Sweaty men labor at their various stations as they:
— cut and sand planks.
— assemble chairs.

NEAR THE OFFICE DOOR: Grandfather sits on a bench as he
watches the workers. Jeffrey stands near.

> JEFFREY
> We'll ship these all out tomorrow. It's the
> final order before church camp.

> GRANDFATHER
> I'm staying in town this summer.

                          JEFFREY
          Brother Keaton, the real heat is about to
          settle in. Should go to the mountains. It's
          much cooler up there.

                        GRANDFATHER
          I prefer to stay.

                          JEFFREY
          Mildred will stay here for Charlotte.

                        GRANDFATHER
          As if she is needed.

Jeffrey considers, turns to the office.

OFFICE - MOMENTS LATER

Dennis does paperwork at the desk.

Jeffrey stands before the desk.

                          JEFFREY
          Just them in town? For weeks?

                          DENNIS
          Can't make him go. They have food, and water.
          It's all they need.

EXT. ALLEN'S BACK DOOR - DAY

The door opens. A shotgun is held by Allen as he somberly
steps out to the bright sun. He pauses as he overlooks...

his property with its perfectly tended vegetable garden
and small orchard next to a barn.

A horse it tied to a water trough beneath a shade tree.

Alan closes the door behind him and stares at the gun.

The horse quietly watches as...

Allen continues to stare at the gun.

EXT. CHURCH — DAY

Wooden boxes of food supplies are carried by sweaty church
members who load the boxes onto a flatbed truck.

Other men load pickup trucks with more supply boxes.

Some women and the few boys file into a big, old bus.

BESIDE MILDRED'S CAR: Unhappy Ruth is shaded by her umbrella as stern Mildred, also with an umbrella, stands near her.

BESIDE THE BUS: The seven teenage girls obediently carry long, white dresses on wire hangers as they board the bus.

One tearful girl stops, turns to her Mother, who won't have it, and guides the hesitant girl onto the bus.

Ruth draws impatient as her eyes plead Mildred.

>   **RUTH**
>   Why can't I go?

Ruth defiantly marches toward the bus.

Mildred drops her umbrella, goes after Ruth, grabs her arm, and pulls her toward the car.

>   **RUTH**
>   (tearfully squeals)
>   Ow. Ow. Ow.

Mildred shoves Ruth into the car, tosses in her umbrella, slams the door.

INT. THE CAR - CONT.

Mildred reaches in and smacks Ruth, who screams in tears.

>   **MILDRED**
>   You cannot be trusted. You little bitch.

Ruth whimpers as she curls up against the opposite door.

Mildred storms over to the tossed umbrella.

THE CAR: Ruth's whimpers as she sits up to watch.

INT. THE CHURCH BUS - CONT.

Jeffrey steps in, and takes the driver's seat. Concerned, he turns and eyes the...

passengers, who converse in hushed tones.

One of the teenage girls weeps.

EXT. THE FLATBED TRUCK/CHURCH PARKING LOT - CONT.

A canvas tarp is spread over boxes of food supplies.

Dennis and other men secure the tarp with ropes.

Shaded by her umbrella, Mildred approaches Dennis as he ties the tarp rope.

                    MILDRED
          You have not tried enough to persuade him. He's
          too elderly to suffer the heat.

He steps to his car as she follows him. He gets in.

                    DENNIS
          If there are any problems, gather them, and
          drive up to camp.

                    MILDRED
          At least take the boy.

Dennis starts the engine.

Jeffrey approaches.

Dennis waves Mildred away. She defiantly waits.

                    DENNIS
          I must speak with Brother Jeffrey.

Mildred sneers and heads to her car.

                    JEFFREY
               (to Dennis)
          Brother Allen hasn't arrived.

Dennis looks about the trucks and bus, as...

men get in the pickup trucks. Engines start.

                    DENNIS
          I'll stop by his residence. Perhaps he needs
          some encouragement.

Jeffrey returns to the bus.

The cars, bus, flatbed truck, and pickup trucks form a
caravan, and pull out to the road. Dust kicks up as they
head toward the mountains.

Dennis' car heads in the opposite direction.

INT. MILDRED'S CAR

Ruth remains huddled in the back seat.

Mildred gets in behind the wheel, slams the door, glares
at Ruth, and starts the engine.

EXT. ALLEN'S HOUSE - LATER - DAY

WOODEN DOOR SIGN: "Henceforth, evil, be gone!"

Dennis steps up to the porch. Knocks on the door. Waits.

INT. ALLEN'S LIVING ROOM - MOMENTS LATER

Dennis enters. Surveys the tidy room appointed with basic wooden furniture.

>   **DENNIS**
>   Brother Allen?

KITCHEN

The open box of shotgun rounds is on the table with a few rounds scattered about.

Dennis factors them as if to calculate the possibilities.

EXT. ALLEN'S BACKYARD - MOMENTS LATER

The horse drinks from the trough beneath the shade tree.

Dennis looks about the landscape.

There is commotion on the far side of the fruit trees.

Dennis looks about the trees and is halted.

A couple of buzzards rip at the flesh of Allen's corpse next to the shotgun.

NEARBY ROCKY BRUSH AREA

Sweaty Dennis drags the corpse by an ankle.

He stops on the far side of a boulder, and drops the ankle.

He uses his foot to shove the corpse and it rolls down into a weedy gully.

GRAVEL

A tree branch is dragged by Dennis to brush away his foot prints.

He stops beside his car, and tosses the branch into the scrub brush.

INT. KEATON DINING ROOM - DAY

Mildred, Samuel, and Grandfather eat lunch.

                    MILDRED
          I can drive you up --

                  GRANDFFATHER
          -- I'm staying here.

                    MILDRED
          But, Father, the heat is --

                  GRANDFFATHER
          -- I am aware of the heat, Mildred.

KITCHEN

Charlotte eats at the table across from Ruth.

The door opens. Mildred enters, and steps up to Ruth.

                    MILDRED
               (to Ruth)
          We're leaving.

Ruth uses a napkin to wipe her mouth.

                    MILDRED
          Hurry up.

Ruth dutifully gets up and exits as Mildred follows out
the back door.

Samuel cautiously enters.

                    SAMUEL
               (whispers)
          Can we go to cold air?

Charlotte puts her finger to her mouth to quiet him.

They listen to the sound of the car doors closing. The
engine is heard revving.

EXT. KEATON CHICKEN COOP PEN - DAY

Chickens peck at seeds scattered by...

Samuel as he watches them eat.

INT. KEATON LIVING ROOM

Grandfather naps on the sofa, mouth agape.

EXT. KEATON SIDE YARD/HORSE CORRAL - LATER

Charlotte cranks the water pump, to fill the horse trough.
The horse drinks.

Charlotte gathers her dress to her thighs, steps into the trough, sits on the side.

Samuel pets the horse.

Charlotte and Samuel hear something and turn to look.

FROM THE ROAD

Amelia drives up in her dusty car.

She stops near the tree, cuts the engine, and steps from the car in a blouse and jeans, and another silken scarf tied around her neck.

Charlotte's eyes fill with nervousness.

> **AMELIA**
> I thought everyone would be at church camp.

She looks about the garden, orchard, and chicken coop.

> **AMELIA**
> Town's smaller than I remember. Some of the houses are rotting... But then, this place has always been rotting.

> **CHARLOTTE**
> (softly, to Samuel)
> Quietly sit on the porch. Don't wake Grandfather.

Samuel bashfully makes his way to the back porch steps. Sits. Watches.

> **CHARLOTTE**
> You must not be here. Mildred is in town.

> **AMELIA**
> And Ruth?

> **CHARLOTTE**
> She's with Mildred.

> **AMELIA**
> Why aren't you at church camp?

> **CHARLOTTE**
> I must repent.

> **AMELIA**
> For what?... Going to the diner?

> **CHARLOTTE**
> I have done many wrong things.

                    AMELIA
You are young and innocent.

                    CHARLOTTE
I am not.

Charlotte looks to...

THE PORCH STEPS: Samuel fidgets with a stick.

Charlotte grasps her baby bump, as if pained.

                    AMELIA
Kicking?

Charlotte nods as she waits for the pain to subside.

                    CHARLOTTE
          (whispers)
Do you know how I can get rid of this baby?

Amelia kneels before Charlotte.

                    AMELIA
It's too late for that, Charlotte. The baby's
too big.

Charlotte covers her face in despair.

                    AMELIA
Charlotte.

Charlotte keeps her hands over her face as she cries.

                    AMELIA
You can't hurt yourself. Samuel needs you.

Charlotte wipes her reddened face and looks to Samuel.

                    AMELIA
          (takes her hand)
I'll help you.

Charlotte appears unsure.

                    CHARLOTTE
Is it true, what you said?

                    AMELIA
About?

                    CHARLOTTE
Your mother taking your baby.

AMELIA
Ruth is my daughter. I wouldn't lie about that.

Charlotte processes this.

CHARLOTTE
(looks around)
If Mildred sees you here.

Amelia dips her hands in the trough and splashes her arms. She stands and scans the sun baked hills.

AMELIA
It's so hot. Reminds me of the day... It was a hot day.

Amelia drifts off in thought.

Charlotte's anxiety gathers as she fidgets.

AMELIA
Bakersfield. It was even hotter there. They left me in Bakersfield.

CHARLOTTE
Amelia. Please. You must leave. If they see you...

AMELIA
They gave me a purse with cash in it. I didn't know what cash was. Like you, now. There were so many things I didn't understand. A shy man helped me buy a bus ticket to Los Angeles. I'm lucky he didn't rob me.

CHARLOTTE
Please, Amelia. If she sees you.

AMELIA
I got a job at a men's club...
(scoffs)
Funny name for it. Men's club. Where they can have their way with young women.

She looks to Charlotte, as if for a glint of understanding.

AMELIA
My breasts were still large from the baby. Men liked it.
(looks to Charlotte)
I became a whore. You know what that means, don't you?

Charlotte barely nods.

                    AMELIA
          Some were police officers. Some were
          politicians. One man had a wife in a wheel
          chair. I actually didn't mind him so much. He
          was kind... Some were preacher men, with their
          church money. Lousy. Usually... Some were
          cruel. Like these God-fearing, righteous men in
          Haven.

Amelia looks to the church steeple in the distance.

                    AMELIA
          "Let those without sin cast the first stone."
          They like that scripture. Makes 'em feel
          better.

She squints as she looks out to the hills.

                    AMELIA
          I haven't seen Father since before the
          accident. They wouldn't let me see him. Is he
          still up in that little house?

                    CHARLOTTE
          You might not want to see him.

                    AMELIA
          You say that because his face? The scars. I
          heard. I saw a lotta' things in prison. There's
          not much left to shock me.

                    CHARLOTTE
          He tends to everyone's horses. And waters
          gardens. Nobody speaks to him... He can't...
          Speak.

Amelia returns to the car. Gets in. Starts the engine.

                    AMELIA
          Come to the diner. Don't let Nancy run you off.
          She's harmless.

Amelia drives away.

Charlotte ponders.

Samuel steps over, sits next to her, and rests his head on
her shoulder.

                    SAMUEL
          Are you going to leave, like Grandmother Keaton
          did?

She puts her arm around his shoulders, brings him close,
her eyes calculating as she holds him.

INT. KEATON LIVING ROOM - CONT.

Grandfather looks out of the screen door. He watches...

EXT. KEATON HOUSE/ROAD - CONT.

Amelia's car drives off as it kicks up dust.

INT. KEATON LIVING ROOM - MINUTES LATER - DAY

Charlotte enters from the dining room, and halts.

Grandfather turns to look at her.

> **GRANDFATHER**
> Dinner is soon, isn't it?

> **CHARLOTTE**
> Yes, Grandfather.

He passes Charlotte, as he goes to sit at the table.

KITCHEN

A pot of cut potatoes is filled with water by Charlotte.

She places it on a burner.

From a pile of cut wood in the corner, she takes a piece, and grabs some pine needles from a wooden box.

She opens the door of the potbellied stove, places the pine needles and the wood inside.

Strikes a match, places it in with the needles, which alight.

EXT. ISAIAH'S HOUSE - DAY

Isaiah pumps water from a well into a bucket near the vegetable garden. He turns to the...

ROAD: Amelia's car parks and she steps out.

> **AMELIA**
> Father.

Isaiah drops the bucket, hobbles into the house, closes the door.

Amelia steps up the gravel path.

> **AMELIA**
> Father.

71

She waits. Looks around at the vegetable garden.

INT. ISAIAH'S LIVING ROOM - CONT.

Sweat builds on Isaiah's forehead, his eyes pained as he stands against the door in the sadly furnished room.

>   AMELIA (O.S.)
>   I've come back for her.

His eyes well.

OUTSIDE THE DOOR

Amelia stands near.

>   AMELIA
>   Father. I forgive you. I've always forgiven
>   you.

She waits. Nothing but silence.

INSIDE THE DOOR

Isaiah listens to Amelia's footsteps fade, the car door shut, the engine crank, and the car pull away.

He wipes away tears as he goes to a window, pulls aside the curtains to see...

the car drive away down the road.

INT. KEATON DINING ROOM - DUSK

OPEN WINDOWS: The sun low near the distant mountains.

Samuel eats across from...

sweaty Grandfather, who stares at his food. He wipes sweat from his forehead.

Mildred also sits at the table. Sweat streaks her face as she considers Grandfather.

>   MILDRED
>   (as if entertained)
>   Are you not feeling well, Father?

His eyes wearily glide to her, and stop. Not amused.

>   MILDRED
>   You decided to stay in this heat.

He defiantly takes up his fork, and eats.

                    GRANDFATHER
          (loudly)
     I need lemon.

As if humored by his misery, Mildred eats.

Charlotte enters with a bowl of cut lemons, places them on
the table, and waits.

                    GRANDFATHER
     That will be all.

Charlotte returns to the kitchen.

He squeezes a lemon wedge into his water and drinks.

                    SAMUEL
          (to Grandfather)
     When is Father returning?

                    MILDRED
     He'll visit, soon.

                    GRANDFATHER
          (glares at Mildred)
     He asked me. Not you.

Mildred dismissively eats. Grandfather drinks water.

Samuel observes them.

KITCHEN

Ruth eats at the table with Charlotte.

                    RUTH
          (whispers)
     Uncle Timothy said that one day I would meet my
     Mother. Doesn't he know who my Mother is?

                    CHARLOTTE
          (whispers)
     Of course he does.

                    RUTH
          (whispers)
     Mother slapped him when he said that.

Charlotte hears something, places her finger to her lips
to hush Ruth.

DOOR: Opens. Mildred suspiciously eyes them as they eat.
Mildred exits.

                              RUTH
                         (whispers)
                    Where did Aunt Marie go?

                              CHARLOTTE
                         (whispers)
                    I don't know. She took the children.

                              RUTH
                         (whispers)
                    That's why Uncle Timothy is around more often?
                    Isn't he? Because Aunt Marie left him? Just
                    like Grandmother Keaton?

                              CHARLOTTE
                         (whispers)
                    We should not gossip. Let us eat.

Ruth's eyes remain curious.

EXT. KEATON HOUSE - LATER - DAY

Mildred's car drives away.

INT. BATHROOM - NIGHT

Eyes closed, Charlotte reclines in a tub of soapy water
with lit candles on the edge of the tub. She stares.

INT. GENERAL STORE - DAY

The food shelves are empty.

At the counter, Timothy bags up household goods, but stops
as he hears a car outside. He looks to the windows.

INT./EXT. MILDRED'S CAR/GENERAL STORE - CONT.

Mildred sits watch in the driver's seat. Ruth is in the
passenger seat. Nearby is Timothy's truck.

                              RUTH
                    Is Uncle Timothy --

                              MILDRED
                    -- Shut up.

STORE: Timothy exits with a filled grocery bag.

                              MILDRED
                    What is it you are doing?

                              TIMOTHY
                    Why aren't you at camp?

                               74

He places the bag in the truck.

> **RUTH**
> Charlotte and Samuel are at home, too.

> **MILDRED**
> (smacks Ruth)
> Shut up!

Ruth's cheek reddens as tears well in her eyes.

> **TIMOTHY**
> Don't you hit —

> **MILDRED**
> (to Timothy)
> -- You're stealing.

> **TIMOTHY**
> Who are you to accuse?

Ruth reaches for the door. Mildred pulls her back, presses on the gas, and speeds away.

Timothy watches the car.

EXT. KEATON DRIVEWAY - DAY

Mildred pulls Ruth by the arm from the car, slams the door, and marches Ruth toward the house.

NEXT TO THE HOUSE: Charlotte stands near the damaged metal framed chicken wire screen of the crawl space.

> **MILDRED**
> (to Ruth)
> Go wait in the house.

Ruth obeys as frustrated Mildred marches up to Charlotte.

> **MILDRED**
> (the bent screen)
> What's this about?

> **CHARLOTTE**
> Raccoons must have torn it open.

Mildred surveys the screen.

Timothy's truck pulls up. He cuts the engine. Steps out.

> **MILDRED**
> What are you doing here?

He approaches as he notices the bent screen.

CHARLOTTE
Raccoons.

TIMOTHY
(fidgets with the screen)
They like the crawl space. It's cooler under
there.

He goes to the truck.

MILDRED
(to Charlotte)
Go in the house.

Charlotte turns as Timothy removes tools from the truck.

TIMOTHY
She doesn't need to go anywhere.

Charlotte stops.

Timothy goes to the crawl space with a tool box.

MILDRED
She should do as I say.

TIMOTHY
She should not.

He kneels near the screen and digs out a nail.

MILDRED
Nobody asked for your help.

He nails the screen shut. Stands.

TIMOTHY
(points with the hammer)
You should leave.

MILDRED
I'm here for dinner.

He puts tools back in the truck.

TIMOTHY
Maybe I'm here for dinner.
(to Charlotte)
May I visit Samuel?

Mildred stands aghast as Charlotte hesitantly nods.

Timothy goes up the front steps and enters the house.

Mildred fumes as she passes Charlotte, and up the steps.

76

Charlotte follows.

INT. KEATON DINING ROOM - MINUTES LATER - DAY

Samuel watches Timothy seated near him across from...

displeased Mildred who glares at Timothy.

Grandfather enters, and pauses.

> TIMOTHY
> Hello, Father.

Grandfather diverts his eyes as he sits.

Charlotte places platters of food on the table next to serving utensils, then exits to the kitchen.

Timothy takes up the utensils.

> MILDRED
> We say grace.

Timothy digs in to the platter and puts food on Samuel's plate, then on his own.

> TIMOTHY
> Because you're holy? Shouldn't you be in the kitchen?

Mildred disgustedly bows her head in silent prayer.

Samuel and Grandfather do the same. Samuel peeks to see...

Timothy eat. He winks at Samuel.

Done with the silent prayer, Mildred takes the serving utensils and puts food onto Grandfather's plate.

> GRANDFATHER
> I can serve myself.

Mildred puts down the serving utensils.

Grandfather takes them, and scoops food onto his plate.

KITCHEN

Charlotte eats dinner with Ruth. Eyes curious as they listen to the voices from the other room.

DINING ROOM - MINUTES LATER

Timothy finishes. Gets up. Takes his plate and utensils.

                    TIMOTHY
        It was nice joining you lovely people for
        dinner.

Samuel leisurely eats.

Timothy exits to the kitchen. Mildred pauses to listen.

KITCHEN

Timothy rinses his plate at the sink, then places it on
the drying cloth.

                    TIMOTHY
        Thank you for dinner, Charlotte.

                    CHARLOTTE
        You're welcome.

Ruth shyly watches him.

                    TIMOTHY
             (nods at)
        Ruth.

He exits out the back door.

DINING ROOM

Mildred goes to the kitchen door, pushes it open, peeks
in, closes it. Sits back at the table.

                    MILDRED
             (to Samuel)
        How many times did you go with your Mother to
        visit Amelia?

Samuel fidgets.

                    GRANDFATHER
        Leave him alone.

                    MILDRED
        It's a simple question.

                    GRANDFATHER
        You leave him alone.

Grandfather glares at her.

                    MILDRED
             (to Samuel)
        How many times did you go --

Grandfather swings his cane at Mildred, who nearly falls
from her chair.

> MILDRED
> (stands and backs away)
> Father! I am not a child!

KITCHEN

The door swings open as Mildred storms in.

Mildred pulls Ruth from her chair, but Ruth holds on.

> MILDRED
> (smacks Ruth)
> Let go!

Ruth explodes in tears.

> MILDRED
> (sneers at Charlotte)
> If you weren't with child.

Charlotte stands and frightfully backs away toward the
dining room door. Samuel enters and grasps onto her.

Grandfather with his cane, pushes past them.

> GRANDFATHER
> (to Mildred)
> Henceforth. Be gone --

> MILDRED
> -- You have no power over me.

Mildred pulls whimpering Ruth out the back door.

EXT. BACK PORCH - DAY - CONT.

Ruth flees down the stairs.

Mildred stops to look disgustedly at the cage of mice.

Grandfather steps out of the door as Mildred storms down
the porch steps.

INT. KITCHEN - DAY - CONT.

Charlotte stands with Samuel as Grandfather enters, passes
them as he returns to the dining room.

> GRANDFATHER (O.S.)
> I would like a baked apple.

Samuel steps aside as Charlotte takes an apple from a bowl and selects the coring tool from the counter.

She cores the apple on the cutting board.

INT. CHURCH CAMP CHAPEL - DAY

An older woman dabs tears from her eyes as she sits in the pews with the other women and children, behind the men who sit in the forward pews.

At the front, seven men (40s-50s), stand dressed in their best rumpled, scuffed suits.

Dennis stands before them, also in a suit.

> **DENNIS**
> (to the seven men)
> I bestow the power of the priesthood. To be a man, with wife. From here and henceforth.

Two young men open the chapel doors.

The veiled seven teenaged girls file down the aisle in simple, full-length white dresses. Their expressions a mix of fright, resilience, pride, and tear-streaks.

The seven men are each joined by a girl, who takes a place beside them. Each couple faces each other.

> **DENNIS**
> The bride gives herself to the groom, to live in his honor, submissive, doing for him as a good wife should...

One groom gently wipes a tear from his bride's cheek.

> **DENNIS**
> ... tending to his needs and desires. To nourish him with foods of our paradise. To mother his children as an honor...

Jeffrey listens in the front row, next to Betty, who stares.

> **DENNIS**
> ...to diligently raise the children into our most blessed flock.

INT. KEATON BARN - DAY

The cow teat is squeezed one last time by Charlotte. She hands the pail to Samuel, who takes it and heads outside.

Charlotte wipes away sweat, unties the cow, grasps the lead, and guides her outside.

EXT. FRONT PORCH - DAY

Grandfather sits as he brushes away a pesky fly.

YARD

Samuel stands near a raven perched on a fence post.

> **SAMUEL**
> (softly)
> Birdie, birdie.

The bird flaps its wings into the sky to join another raven. They glide away into the distance.

Samuel watches as his eyes are full of wonder.

EXT. BACK PORCH - DAY

The mice in the cage scamper about nibbling on seeds and bits of bread as Charlotte watches them with Samuel.

> **SAMUEL**
> Do animals get married?

> **CHARLOTTE**
> No. Only people get married.

> **SAMUEL**
> Why?

Charlotte ponders as she straightens Samuel's hair.

> **CHARLOTTE**
> It's what people do.

She enters the house. Samuel watches the mice.

EXT. CHURCH CAMP CABINS - DAY

An older woman sits on a bench as she fans herself.

A middle-aged man and his teenage bride stroll the pathway.

The bride awkwardly holds onto his arm. She hesitates as he guides her to the door of a small cabin. He takes her arm, pulling her inside. The door closes.

The older woman looks askance, worriedly stares forward.

EXT. FOREST PATHWAY/CHURCH CAMP PARKING AREA - DAY

Betty wanders among the trees. She stops to watch...

a butterfly land on a wildflower.

As she watches the butterfly, she hears conversation. She peeks through an opening in bushes to see...

PARKING AREA

Among pine trees are the bus, pickup trucks, and Dennis' car, where he stands with Jeffrey.

> **DENNIS**
> Conduct the evening service as I would. I will hold council when I return.

> **JEFFREY**
> Will you see Brother Allen? Perhaps he will ride with you back to camp, now that the weddings are completed.

Dennis daringly gazes at Jeffrey. Jeffrey seems unsure.

> **DENNIS**
> Yes, I will visit him.

As Dennis continues to gaze at Jeffrey, Dennis takes Jeffery's hand. Jeffrey appears uncomfortable.

> **JEFFREY**
> What is --

Dennis simply continues to hold his hand and gaze into his eyes.

BEHIND BUSHES

Perplexed, Betty watches.

DENNIS AND JEFFREY

Their breath deepens. Dennis cups the side of Jeffrey's neck. Jeffrey backs away and shakes his head "no."

Dennis gets in the car, starts the engine. Gives one last, longing look as he shifts the car, and drives away to the dirt road through the forest.

In wonder, Jeffrey watches the car drive away.

PATHWAY

Betty flees.

EXT. BEHIND DINER - DAY

Stones land in a dry river bed.

Samuel picks up another stone. Tosses it to the wash.

Beneath the shade tree, Charlotte and Amelia, with another silken neck scarf, sit on a bench near the horse.

> **CHARLOTTE**
> She eats in the kitchen, with me. Mildred eats in the dining room, with Grandfather. He doesn't like it.

> **AMELIA**
> You have her alone in the kitchen every evening?

> **CHARLOTTE**
> (nods)
> She asks when she will be married.

Amelia stands, paces, and huffs in frustration.

> **CHARLOTTE**
> The men whose wives left Haven with their children, and a couple of the widowers were promised wives.

Amelia stops pacing as she listens.

> **CHARLOTTE**
> Thirteen of the younger men left one day. They were given money. I heard Mildred and Minister Dennis speak. Then, the boys who went to the Korea war. With those boys all gone, the widowed men marry girls.

> **AMELIA**
> Had I stayed, I'd be like you.

Charlotte looks out to something in the distance, Amelia follows her eye line to the...

TRUCKSTOP: Timothy's truck stops next to a fuel pump. His door opens. He gets out.

Charlotte and Amelia watch Timothy.

> **CHARLOTTE**
> (to Samuel)
> Get close, now. Near the horse.

Samuel does as told.

> CHARLOTTE
> (to Amelia, RE: Timothy)
> His wife hasn't returned. I'm sure he misses
> his children.

TRUCKSTOP

The station attendant gasses up Timothy's truck.

Timothy stands near as he wipes sweat from his brow.

NEARBY ROAD/DENNIS' CAR...

slows to a stop as he notices...

THROUGH DENNIS' WINDSHIELD: Timothy stands beside his
flatbed truck as the half-busy fuel station.

Dennis contemplates. Looks about. Frustrated, he does a
smooth U-turn and speeds away in the other direction.

TRUCKSTOP

Timothy guzzles water from a glass bottle as he stands
beside his truck. As if he senses eyes on him, he scans
the surroundings. His eyes land on...

CHARLOTTE AND AMELIA BENEATH THE TREE

Charlotte's breath shudders. Amelia looks to her.

> CHARLOTTE
> They're his.

> AMELIA
> What is?

> CHARLOTTE
> My babies. They're Timothy's.

It hits Amelia.

> CHARLOTTE
> Samuel is Timothy's son.

Amelia kneels before her as Charlotte bows her head.

> CHARLOTTE
> Minister Dennis has not known me.
> (she cries)
> I have sinned. I am an adulteress.

> AMELIA
> You've gotta get away from here.

Charlotte cries as she surveys the distance.

                    CHARLOTTE
          I know nothing beyond this horizon. This is as
          far as I've ever traveled.

                    AMELIA
          Things are better away from here.

EXT./INT. HIGHWAY ENTRANCE/DENNIS' CAR - DAY - CONT.

ROAD SIGN: "Sacramento 75. San Francisco 157."

Sweat streaks Dennis' face as he factors the sign while he
sits in the idling car.

EXT. BEHIND DINER - DAY - CONT.

Samuel remains near the horse as he keeps watch.

TRUCKSTOP

GAS PUMP: The register numbers click, counting the gallons
and dollars. It clicks off.

The attendant removes the nozzle.

Timothy pulls out his wallet.

BENEATH SHADE TREE

On the log, Charlotte lightly hyperventilates as Amelia
sits beside her and holds her hand.

                    SAMUEL
               (approaches)
          What's the matter, Mother?

                    AMELIA
          She'll be okay. Stay near the horse, please.

Samuel does as told, the horse bows its head. He pets it.

                    AMELIA
          I saw Ruth for the first time two months ago.
          Here, at the gas station. One time, our eyes
          met. It seemed like magic.

They notice as Timothy approaches.

                    TIMOTHY
          Hello, Amelia. You look much older.

                         AMELIA
                       (coldly)
            Hello, Uncle Timothy.

                         TIMOTHY
            It's time to take care of some matters.

Amelia waits.

                         TIMOTHY
            Isn't that what you came back for?

She offers no indication.

                         TIMOTHY
            There's a wedding in those mountains this week.
            Next year, it could be Ruth... Or, the year
            after.

                         AMELIA
            Why didn't you do something about it?

                         TIMOTHY
            Like what? Call the law? Of all people, you
            trust the law?

Amelia stands, as if about to burst with anger.

                         CHARLOTTE
                       (gets between them)
            No. No. No... No. Please.

Amelia turns away as she recomposes.

                         TIMOTHY
            Mildred'll be at dinner. With Ruth. Won't she,
            Charlotte?

Amelia looks to Charlotte, who nods.

                         TIMOTHY
                       (to Charlotte)
            Make dinner tonight. As usual. Don't do
            anything differently.

Amelia's cold look to Timothy fades into realization as
she turns to Charlotte, who thoughtfully nods.

Timothy approaches Samuel and crouches down.

                         TIMOTHY
            Be a good boy. Don't tell Mildred or
            Grandfather any of this.

Samuel looks to Charlotte, who nods.

                              86

                    TIMOTHY
If Mildred asks you anything, simply stay
quiet. Don't say a word. Not even one word.
Don't say anything.

Timothy reassuringly pats Samuel's shoulder.

                    TIMOTHY
          (to Charlotte and Amelia)
See you at the house.

Timothy goes back to the truck.

BACK SERVICE DOOR OF DINER

Nancy slightly opens the door to watch.

Then goes back inside as the door creaks shut.

AMELIA AND CHARLOTTE

They gaze across the road, to the...

JUNK YARD: Dominated by the mangled church bus.

The gravity of thought draws Charlotte's face. Amelia
guides her to sit with her on the log.

                    AMELIA
I think of it. Always.

Charlotte looks to Amelia as she gathers her thoughts.

                    AMELIA
Mother didn't want me going to camp. I was
supposed to stay hidden. She wore the folded
towel beneath her dress. She planned on sending
me to camp the next year. To be married, as if
I was pure.

Samuel approaches.

                    AMELIA
          (to Samuel)
Just a minute, honey. You stay with the horse a
little longer, now.

Samuel picks some dry grass and feeds the horse.

Amelia considers Charlotte's baby bump.

                    AMELIA
When Father shoved me onto the bus, people
noticed my baby bump. They looked at me with
shame. Father jumped in the driver seat. I
yelled at him to stop.

They notice

NEAR THE DINER: Timothy's truck parks. He gets out and
walks to the diner.

Amelia stares at the ground.

                    AMELIA
We got on the mountain road, and Mother drove
her car around the side of the bus. Everyone
was hollering and screaming.

Amelia stops to ponder.

                    AMELIA
I woke up on the mountainside. Bodies were
scattered. I heard Father moan. I couldn't tell
where he was. Mother ran down and pulled me up
the hill. I didn't know my neck was bleeding.

Amelia stares at the distance as Charlotte watches her.

                    AMELIA
Maybe people would blame me.

Amelia pulls down the pretty scarf on her neck to reveal a
terrible scar. Charlotte winces.

                    AMELIA
              (feels the scar)
Every day, this reminds me that all those
people died. And I didn't.

She readjusts the scarf over the scar.

                    AMELIA
I didn't want her to take my baby.

                    CHARLOTTE
We must do this.

Charlotte stands, and picks up her umbrella.

                    CHARLOTTE
You must be very quiet. Park down the road. No
place near the house, or she'll hear you. Make
sure her car's parked out front. Go to the back
kitchen door.

Charlotte helps Samuel onto the horse. She hands him the umbrella, then gets up onto the horse in front of him.

She guides the horse toward the hills.

Amelia thoughtfully walks back to the diner. A thought hits her, her pace picks up, determined.

INT. DINER - DAY

COUNTER SEAT: Timothy finishes his meal.

Amelia approaches the counter and places dirty plates on a cart. She turns to...

Timothy, who waits as she factors him.

> **AMELIA**
> Charlotte told me.

His eyes don't care.

> **AMELIA**
> Uncle Dennis doesn't have children.

She gives him time. His expression unmoved.

ACROSS THE DINER

Nancy cleans a table as she watches...

AMELIA AND TIMOTHY AT THE COUNTER

She continues to face him.

> **TIMOTHY**
> Are you without sin?

She looks him over.

> **AMELIA**
> Samuel does look more like you.

COOK'S WINDOW: Bobby places plates of food on the shelf, and dings the bell.

Amelia takes up the plates of food, glances knowingly at Timothy, then carries the food to customers.

Timothy places cash on the counter as he gets up.

EXT. BRUSHLAND HILLSIDE - LATER - DAY

The horse trots quickly as sweaty Charlotte sits in front as Samuel behind her holds up the umbrella. They reach the hill crest.

Charlotte stops the horse as they look out at...

THE VIEW: Haven roasts in the sun beneath the forested mountains.

Charlotte wipes sweat from her face and motions for the horse to continue. Samuel holds on tight as they move along.

EXT./INT. DINER/TIMOTHY'S TRUCK - DAY

Timothy strides to the truck, gets in. Starts the engine. He settles into a thoughtful stare toward the...

JUNKYARD: The mangled bus sits among the bashed and rusted cars and pickup trucks.

Timothy continues to stare, lost in memories.

INT. DINER KITCHEN SERVICE WINDOW - CONT.

Nancy eyes...

Amelia who changes the coffee filter as Bobby listens.

> **NANCY**
> (to Amelia)
> What exactly is your relationship with those people?

Amelia glances to Bobby, who watches expectantly. She finishes with the coffee filter.

> **AMELIA**
> (to Nancy)
> Charlotte has had enough of her husband, Minister Dennis. He's my uncle. Charlotte is my aunt. The boy is my cousin.

Nancy is baffled.

> **AMELIA**
> You asked.

Amelia picks up a plate of food from the cook's window and carries it away.

                    NANCY
               (to Bobby)
     You know she was in prison, don't you?

                    BOBBY
     Amelia? For what?

                    NANCY
     Don't you think she's awfully flirtatious with
     these truckers?

Nancy takes a plate of food to a customer.

Bobby watches...

ACROSS THE DINER: Amelia giggles at something the trucker
says. The trucker smiles as he checks her out.

Bobby factors the situation. Gives up. Flips burgers.

EXT. GABRIEL'S FARM STAND - DAY

Two big watermelons are carried by a man to his car, where
his children and wife wait.

Gabriel stands watch as Timothy selects vegetables and a
watermelon, and places them in a box.

                    GABRIEL
     Two, even. Sound about right?

Timothy pulls cash from his wallet and hands it over.

                    TIMOTHY
     Don't know what the town would do without your
     brother taking care of the animals. How can he
     have it in him to do anything for them?

                    GABRIEL
     Best to let bygones be.

Timothy picks up the box.

                    TIMOTHY
     If your family got the church back --

                    GABRIEL
     -- You know Minister Isaiah gave it to Mildred
     for what he did.

                    TIMOTHY
     Gave it? Or, she took it? And gave it to
     Dennis. As if he wanted it... Besides, we know
     who caused the accident.

Dismissively, Gabriel continues to pack up for the day.

>   TIMOTHY
> Why didn't you find a new wife after the
> accident?... Or, leave this place?

>   GABRIEL
> I am my brother's keeper. Where else could he
> go, looking like that? With people staring
> everywhere he goes.

>   TIMOTHY
> Secrets usually don't remain unspoken.

Timothy carries the box to his truck.

>   TIMOTHY
>   (turns back)
> The kingdom will be yours.

Timothy gets in the truck, and drives away.

Gabriel watches.

EXT. CHURCH HORSE CORRAL - DAY

The trough beneath the shade tree is filled with water
pumped by Isaiah. Finished, he pets a horse.

ROAD

Shaded by the umbrella Samuel holds as he sits behind her
on the horse, Charlotte slows the horse to a stop.

SHADE TREE: Isaiah looks on as....

Charlotte approaches as a couple horses drink from the
trough. She looks to him.

>   CHARLOTTE
> It's your penance to take care of the animals.
> Isn't it, Minister Isaiah?

She watches as he grabs the scoop from the feed bin.

>   CHARLOTTE
> Amelia told me about how the accident
> happened... And about Ruth.

He scatters a scoop of oats into the feeder and secures
the lid of the bin. Finally, slightly nods yes.

The horses approach and eat.

He and Charlotte watch them.

                         CHARLOTTE
          None of us are without sin.

He shakes his head.

                         CHARLOTTE
          I do not blame you, Minister. It was not your
          fault.

Samuel remains on the horse. Charlotte gets on in front of
him, he holds up the umbrella.

Isaiah grabs a pitch fork and breaks apart a bale of hay.
Forks some over to a horse that munches.

Isaiah looks about, falls to his knees, and deeply cries.

EXT. SAN FRANCISCO HILL VIEWPOINT - DAY

A grand distant view of the city and Golden Gate bridge.

Dennis, long sleeves rolled up, his shirt untucked, he
sits on the hood of his car while gazing at...

the view of the city.

Thoughts gather in his eyes that shift to notice, a...

NEARBY DIRT TRAIL: A young, handsome, shirtless man stands
alone.

Another man casually approaches. They demurely check out
each other. One heads off deeper into the trail. The other
man follows.

Dennis slyly observes.

EXT. KEATON YARD - DAY

Samuel climbs onto a wooden fence and balances as he steps
along the top beam. Nearly loses balance. Regains it. He
stops as he sees...

ON THE GROUND: A cat skeleton bakes in the sun.

Samuel hops down from the fence.

His foot nudges the cat skull. It rolls in the scorched
dirt.

INT. KEATON KITCHEN - CONT.

A pot of beans is stirred by Charlotte, her face sweaty.

EXT. KEATON FRONT YARD - MINUTES LATER

Twine is tied around the cat skull by Samuel.

He picks up the end of the string and...

twirls the skull around in circles over his head.

Around and around the cat skull twirls. Around and around.

DRIVEWAY: Mildred pulls up in her car. She and Ruth exit. Mildred stops to watch as...

SAMUEL: Continues to twirl the cat skull above his head as he stares back at...

MILDRED: As if disturbed, she looks away and continues to the porch.

Ruth follows Mildred as she watches...

Samuel stare at Mildred as he twirls the cat skull.

EXT. SIDE OF HAVEN GENERAL STORE - CONT.

Sun-scorched gravel. A wet red fleshy chunk of watermelon lands. Steam from the red wetness rises.

A desert tortoise approaches. Sniffs the melon chunk. Bites in.

Timothy sits on the back of his flatbed truck as he eats watermelon. Tosses another piece to the tortoise.

He looks about at the sound of a car.

ROAD: Amelia's car passes.

INT. CHARLOTTE'S BEDROOM/HALLWAY - CONT.

The alarm clock ticks. Tick. Tick. Tick. Tick.

Charlotte stands at the doorway as she stares at...

the two beds divided by the veil of fabric hung from the ceiling.

DINING ROOM

The table set. Mildred sits and waits. She takes her napkin and dabs sweat from her forehead. The sounds of Grandfather's cane and steps are heard.

He stops in the doorway. Displeasure crosses his face. He continues forward to sit in his chair. They wait.

Samuel enters. He sits at the table.

Mildred eyes...

Samuel, who stares back.

> **MILDRED**
> This boy knows things. Don't you, Samuel?

Samuel continues to stare at her.

> **GRANDFATHER**
> You leave him alone.

Mildred places the napkin on her lap.

Samuel, also places his napkin on his lap. Waits.

Mildred, who suspiciously studies him.

EXT. COLLAPSED HOUSE - CONT.

Beneath a shade tree, Amelia leans on her car while she watches...

DOWN THE ROAD: Mildred's car is parked in front of the Keaton house.

EXT. SAN FRANCISCO'S OCEAN BEACH - CONT.

Dennis follows a path between the sand dunes to the broad, sandy beach. He stops as he looks out to...

the vast Pacific ocean. The surf glides toward shore.

Dennis gazes at the ocean as the breeze tousles his hair.

INT. KEATON KITCHEN - CONT.

Ruth sits at the table set for two.

At the counter, Charlotte wipes sweat from her brow as she prepares a large platter of food.

DINING ROOM

Mildred, Samuel, and Grandfather watch as Charlotte places the platter on the table.

Charlotte exits to the kitchen.

Mildred, Samuel, and Grandfather bow their heads for silent grace.

PRE-LAP: The sounds of ocean surf rolling in

EXT. SAN FRANCISCO'S OCEAN BEACH - CONT.

The surf rolls in and creeps up to his knees and retreats and his bare feet sink into the sand as...

Dennis is mesmerized by the waves.

INT. KEATON DINING ROOM - CONT.

Samuel eats as...

Mildred suspiciously considers him

Displeased, Grandfather watches her.

KITCHEN

Charlotte looks to the window of the back door as Ruth eats.

EXT. SAN FRANCISCO'S OCEAN BEACH - CONT.

Dennis stands in the surf as he watches...

The sun peek from behind wispy clouds.

NEARBY: A sketchy, muscular YOUNG MAN (30s), with his open shirt billowing in the breeze, which reveals his taut six-pack belly. He eyes...

Dennis, who watches the Young Man meander past him.

The Young Man looks back to see...

Dennis' hungry eyes linger on him.

The Young Man gestures for Dennis to follow.

Taunted, Dennis watches the Young Man walk to the dunes.

INT. KEATON DINING ROOM - CONT.

As they eat.

> **SAMUEL**
> (to Grandfather)
> I found cat bones.

> **MILDRED**
> Don't you say such things at the dinner table.

> **GRANDFATHER**
> Don't you tell him what to do.

Her glare deflects him.

Samuel observes their dynamics.

EXT. HAVEN COLLAPSED HOUSE - CONT.

Amelia stands on the side of the road.

Timothy's truck slows beside her. He cuts the engine.

INT. KEATON KITCHEN - CONT.

As Charlotte and Ruth eat.

>   **RUTH**
>   (whispers)
>   The other girls are getting married. When will
>   I be married?

>   **CHARLOTTE**
>   (whispers)
>   We must be quiet.

Ruth almost speaks.

Charlotte shakes her head, no.

EXT. SAND DUNES - OCEAN BEACH - CONT.

The muscular Young Man sits down in a sand dune area
surrounded by beach grass and ice plant.

Dennis makes his way up the dune from the beach.

The Young Man provocatively pats the sand beside him.

Dennis sits beside the Young Man, who playfully nudges
him. They gaze into each other's eyes.

The Young Man winks. Dennis studies his face.

As Dennis gently moves closer, the Young Man nudges him
away and fidgets with his shirt, to button it.

Dennis reaches out to stop him from buttoning the shirt.

The Young Man undoes the buttons and lounges back onto the
sand. Dennis touches the Young Man's muscular belly.

The Young Man is quickly on top of Dennis, as if playing
rough.

Dennis appears enthralled, until the Young Man grabs
Dennis' neck. Dennis struggles to loosen the iron grip.

                    DENNIS
                  (gasps)
          Henceforth, evil be --

The Young Man intensely squeezes Dennis' neck tighter.

Dennis' face reddens as he struggles to reach for the face
of the Young Man, who chokes Dennis harder.

Dennis tries to pull the hands from his neck. The grip is
too tight.

The Young Man continues as Dennis' reddened eyes strain,
fade, and roll back.

The Young Man holds the grip, as if to be sure. Then
shoves arms full of sand onto Dennis' face and torso.

The Young Man searches Dennis' pockets, and finds the
wallet and car keys.

Dennis' legs move.

The Young Man STOMPS on Dennis' chest, and stands on it.
No more movement, he shoves more sand onto Dennis.

INT. KEATON DINING ROOM - CONT.

Mildred and Grandfather pause, mysteriously confounded.

                    MILDRED
                  (to Grandfather)
          What is it?

Grandfather clears his throat, looks about, then fidgets
with his food, and stops, unsure.

Mildred stands, as if she detects some sort of presence.

                    KITCHEN
          Charlotte stares as Ruth eats. They're startled
          as...

Mildred opens the door. Suspiciously eyes them.

Charlotte and Ruth cautiously look to her.

Mildred exits.

                    RUTH
                  (whispers)
          What is she doing?

Charlotte mildly shakes her head.

LIVING ROOM

Mildred scans the room, as if she senses a disturbance.

DINING ROOM

Samuel and Grandfather watch Mildred.

EXT. OCEAN BEACH - CONT.

As he walks along the surf, the Young Man takes the cash from the wallet, then tosses the wallet into the ocean.

As he walks along, the surf washes away his footprints.

EXT. HAVEN ROAD - CONT.

Timothy sits on the back of his truck as he watches...

Amelia walk along the road toward the Keaton house.

INT. KEATON DINING ROOM - CONT.

Charlotte enters with a platter of baked stuffed apples.

She places it on the table with dessert plates and forks.

> **MILDRED**
> Dessert? This isn't a diner, Charlotte.

> **GRANDFATHER**
> Then, don't eat it.

KITCHEN

Charlotte enters and sees, at the...

BACK DOOR WINDOW: Amelia peeks in.

Charlotte turns to Ruth, puts her finger to her mouth to stay quiet, and gestures for Ruth to follow her.

Ruth hesitantly stands, and cautiously follows Charlotte.

DINING ROOM

Mildred fidgets with her food.

Grandfather scoops a baked apple to a dessert plate.

EXT. KEATON HOUSE - CONT.

Timothy pulls up in the truck, cuts the engine, hops out in time to see...

Ruth follows Amelia as they scurry up the road, Charlotte holds her baby bump as she trails them.

INT. KEATON DINING ROOM - CONT.

Samuel fidgets as Mildred stands and goes to the...

LIVING ROOM

Timothy enters and passes Mildred.

> **MILDRED**
> What are you doing?

She storms behind him as he continues to the...

DINING ROOM

Samuel stands as Timothy enters.

> **TIMOTHY**
> C'mon, son.

Samuel approaches Timothy.

> **MILDRED**
> You don't call him —

> **TIMOTHY**
> -- Shut your mouth.

Mildred blocks Timothy, who grabs her by the arm and she hits him.

> **MILDRED**
> Let go of --

Timothy pushes her. She screams as she falls through the swing door of...

KITCHEN

Mildred falls in against the empty table. Dinner plates and glasses shatter. She cuts her leg on the mess as she struggles to stand.

> **MILDRED**
> (runs to the back door)
> Charlotte! Ruth!

EXT. BACK PORCH - CONT.

Mildred collides with the mouse cage and is tangled with it as she falls down the steps.

She screams as mice scamper away. She struggles to untangle from the crushed cage as her leg bleeds.

INT. KITCHEN - CONT.

Grandfather surveys...

the mess of shattered plates and glasses, and drops of blood.

EXT. FRONT YARD - CONT.

With Samuel in the truck, Timothy drives away.

PORCH

Grandfather steps out to the porch and looks...

UP THE ROAD

Samuel looks out the back window of Timothy's truck.

INT. THE TRUCK (MOVING)

Timothy sees in the...

REAR VIEW MIRROR: Mildred's car speeds up behind him.

Timothy looks...

FAR UP THE ROAD: Ruth and Amelia help Charlotte run as she holds her baby bump.

Ruth looks behind to see...

Timothy's truck speeds far behind as Mildred's car tailgates the truck.

INT. MILDRED'S CAR (MOVING)

Rage in her eyes as she speeds next to the truck.

ROAD

Mildred's car drives out in front of Timothy's truck. She swerves. He swerves and runs over a small tree.

TIMOTHY'S TRUCK (MOVING)

Timothy loses control and puts his arm out to protect Samuel.

The truck spins in the dust.

Mildred's car speeds up the road.

The truck speeds after Mildred's car.

AMELIA'S CAR (PARKED)

Doors slam as Charlotte and Ruth are in the back seat.

Amelia is in the driver's seat, starts the engine.

Charlotte and Ruth look out the back window.

Amelia presses on the gas as she speeds up the road.

Ruth screams and Charlotte reaches out to hold her.

Mildred's car hits the rear bumper. They jolt forward.

Amelia speeds up.

Mildred's eyes rage as she speeds.

Mildred's car again hits Amelia's bumper. Amelia speeds down the center of the road.

Timothy's truck speeds up behind Mildred's car.

Mildred drives alongside Amelia's car.

As Amelia slightly swerves, Mildred's car goes through brush on the side of the road.

INT. TIMOTHY'S TRUCK (MOVING)

Samuel nervously holds onto the door and seat.

ROAD

Amelia slightly swerves to ward off Mildred who speeds alongside her.

Timothy's truck slows.

Amelia swerves again, and nearly hits...

Mildred's car, which swerves into the brushland, spins in the dust, flips, and rolls through scrub brush.

IMT. AMELIA'S CAR (MOVING)

Amelia slows as...

Ruth screams in tears.

They all look out the back window as Amelia stops the car.

BRUSHLAND

Timothy's truck stops near Mildred's flipped car.

Timothy gets out. Samuel opens his door and hops out.

> **TIMOTHY**
> (to Samuel)
> Stay inside.

Samuel retreats into the truck.

Timothy approaches the overturned car.

Amelia's car stops nearby.

Bloodied Mildred crawls from the overturned car and painfully stands against the side of it.

Amelia, Charlotte, and crying Ruth exit their car.

Mildred stumbles toward Ruth.

Amelia steps between them as Mildred falls onto Amelia and grasps Amelia's neck scarf as Mildred falls and pulls down Amelia with her.

Mildred twists Amelia's scarf to choke her as they wrestle, but Mildred won't let go.

> **MILDRED**
> Sinner!

Amelia repeatedly punches Mildred, who loses her grip on the scarf.

Amelia gets up and backs away as she regains her breath.

Mildred stands and limps toward Amelia, who backs away with Charlotte and Ruth.

> **MILDRED**
> Be gone, evil!

Timothy steps between them.

Mildred attempts to smack him. He grabs her arm.

> **MILDRED**
> Damn you!

Mildred falls to her knees as Timothy keeps hold of her arm and leans her against a boulder.

INT. TIMOTHY'S TRUCK (PARKED)

Samuel cries.

Charlotte steps up and takes his hand. She brushes away his tears and leads him to Amelia's car.

> **SAMUEL**
> Where are we going, Mother?

> **CHARLOTTE**
> Far away from here.

> **SAMUEL**
> Heaven?

Charlotte gets Samuel into the front seat of Amelia's car.

> **CHARLOTTE**
> To a better place to live. With Amelia and Ruth.

Mildred watches from where she sits against the boulder.

Ruth cries as Amelia guides Ruth to the car.

Charlotte steps up to Timothy.

> **CHARLOTTE**
> Amelia said there's a house.

> **TIMOTHY**
> In Salinas. A good town, near the ocean. You'll like it there.

> **CHARLOTTE**
> We have never seen the ocean.

Timothy hands Charlotte a small stack of cash. She looks to it as if it is unfamiliar material.

> **TIMOTHY**
> Amelia will teach you.

> **CHARLOTTE**
> What of you?

> **TIMOTHY**
> I'll be leaving here, to a place called Big Sur. Not far from Salinas.

Charlotte gives him a long look. Then, steps away, but turns back to the view of Haven town in the distance.

                        TIMOTHY
            You better be on your way.

Charlotte continues to gaze out at the town.

Amelia approaches Timothy.

                        AMELIA
            Did you give Charlotte the money?

He nods.

Amelia leers at Mildred.

                        AMELIA
                    (to Mildred)
            Goodbye, Mother.

Mildred watches...

Amelia and Charlotte get into the car. Engine revs up.

INSIDE CAR: Charlotte and Ruth watch out the back window
as the car drives away.

TIMOTHY: looks to Mildred as she leans on the boulder.

                        MILDRED
            Minister Dennis will not --

                        TIMOTHY
            -- Has nothing. Is nothing. Neither are you.
            Other than a curse.

He goes to the truck, gets in, and starts the engine.

                        MILDRED
            Don't you leave me here!

He drives away.

Appalled, She struggles to stand.

INT. AMELIA'S CAR - CONT.

Samuel is in the passenger seat as Amelia drives.

BACK SEAT: the wind tousles Ruth's hair. Her face dusty
and tear-streaked, she stares out the window. She breaks
from her stare into frightful concern.

Charlotte assuredly takes her hand.

                        RUTH
            Is Mother going to die?

> AMELIA
> No. She won't die.

Ruth dries her tears on her sleeves. Then, watches...

REARVIEW MIRROR: Amelia's eyes as she drives. She looks to see...

Ruth watch her. Then, her eyes light up.

> RUTH
> (to Amelia)
> I remember you. I saw you in the window, at the truck stop.

Amelia watches in the rearview mirror.

> RUTH
> (to Amelia)
> We have the same color of eyes.

> AMELIA
> Oh, sweetie. You have beautiful eyes. It's a compliment to say mine are like yours.

Ruth gives in to a hint of a smile, as does Charlotte.

Tears streak Amelia's cheeks as she drives, she looks beside her to...

Samuel as he gazes out at the lingering twilight.

EXT. OCEAN BEACH SAND DUNES - DAY

Several concerned people watch and whisper to each other.

Detectives arrive and pass the whispering people.

The detectives continue to where...

Police stand near Dennis's half-buried body.

INT. MONTEREY DINER - KITCHEN - ONE YEAR LATER - DAY

Cake batter is poured into tins by...

Betty, in kitchen whites and her hair tied in a bun.

She takes up the pie tins and places them in the oven.

She picks up the dirty bowl and spatula and passes a...

cook flipping burgers at the grill.

It is Isaiah, in a cook's uniform. He adds more burger patties to the grill.

Betty proceeds to the sink, where she rinses the bowl.

DINER DINING ROOM

A well-dressed woman reads a newspaper at a booth as early 1960s pop music plays.

At the next table, Ruth and Samuel and two other children play checkers and enjoy banana splits.

At another table, a couple looks through a menu.

In a waitress uniform and a silk scarf around her neck, Amelia stands ready to take their order.

CASH REGISTER: Coins are counted by Charlotte, also in a waitress uniform. She hands the change to...

a Man (50s), in a suit. Something is off-kilter about him.

> MAN
> (odd smile)
> You make the best pies.

> CHARLOTTE
> Thank you. We do appreciate the business.

He places a Christian pamphlet on the counter.

> MAN
> I'm the minister of the church on the corner.
> We have sermons every Sunday morning at ten.
> Feel welcome to attend.

She blankly considers him and his posed smile.

> CHARLOTTE
> Have a pleasant evening, sir.

> MAN
> (rejected)
> Thank you, sister.

> CHARLOTTE
> (sternly)
> We're not related, sir.

Denied, he nods goodbye as he steps back, and nearly trips as he exits.

She slides her hand along the counter to nudge the church pamphlet over the edge, into a trash bucket.

She sits at the counter next to where her baby sleeps in a carriage.

A customer enters.

Charlotte stands and approaches.

                      CHARLOTTE
              (to new customer)
      Good evening. Feel free to sit anywhere you'd
      like. The waitress will be right with you.

Charlotte stops at the table where the children play checkers.

Charlotte watches them.

                    THE END

I hope you enjoyed the ride.

And that you can one day watch this film.

The scenes on the silver screen
will be what were at one time my thoughts unseen.

Daniel

The Screenwriter

Daniel John Carey is the founder of the Los Angeles-based Screenwriting Tribe screenplay incubation workshop for writers helping writers.

Carey also is the author of the *Screenplay Repair Manual*. The book has been used as a text in film schools. It was written to go along with David Trottier's *The Screenwriter's Bible*. Those interested in writing screenplays are encouraged to study both books, and apply what they learn to their screenplays, before submitting the screenplays to managers, agents, producers, development executives, and others in the industry.

If you have enjoyed the screenplay,
please write a customer review on Amazon
to entice others to partake.

www.ingramcontent.com/pod-product-compliance
Lightning Source LLC
Chambersburg PA
CBHW081207170626
46811CB00011B/3333